Last Whispers of War:

An American Soldier and an ISIS Terrorist Alone in the Desert

by Neal Bogosian

Also by Neal Bogosian

FICTION

The Adventures of Chip Doolin (2011)

NONFICTION

The Age of Healing:
Profiles from an Energy Healer (2015)

You can also see Neal at www.LearnitLive.com

Last Whispers of War:

An American Soldier and an ISIS Terrorist Alone in the Desert

by Neal Bogosian

FAISIA
PUBLISHING

Published and distributed by: Faisia Publishing
Paperback and digital editions 2016

Back cover photo by: Denise Rafkind,
Denise Rafkind Photography

Cover design by: Rob Allen @n23art

This is a work of fiction. Names, characters, places, and
incidents either are the product of the author's
imagination or are used fictitiously. Any resemblance to
actual persons, living or dead, events, or locales is
entirely coincidental.

The author and publisher are in no way liable for any
misuse of the material. Any application of the material
set forth in the following pages is at the reader's
discretion and is his or her sole responsibility.

ISBN-13: 978-0692685334 (Faisia Publishing)

ISBN-10: 0692685332

Acknowledgements

To Andy McWain, your friendship reignited the creative spark in me, for which I thank you – you are a good man! Thanks also to Denise Rafkind of *Denise Rafkind Photography*, for your generous and amazing photo shoot; Faisia Publishing, and my mother and father, for your constant unwavering support – I love you both.

Their journey brought back memories of my autistic brother. I reflected on the intricacies of my own growth and revelation – the patience required in the process of understanding. What we experience is relative and personal. It is about opening our eyes to more...the bigger picture of it all; to remove the veil that shrouds our true potential, both individually and as a civilization. Thank you for the reminder. I love you, brother.

To all of those who seek peace, and who can conceive of a better world without ego, let it be so...let us all visualize that world full of light, and resonate on that same frequency.

Perhaps our visions shall manifest – it has begun!

I kept telling myself…that even in hate there can be hope, for what is my individual faith, but the differing perceptions of others; it is relative to only my own.

-- Journal entry written by
the ISIS soldier from Palestine

I soon learned…that even in chaos – of the mind and of the world – there can be calm. It is where the 'underneath' of life is found – the real substance that is within all of us.

-- Journal entry written by
the American soldier

It is unknown what ultimately became of these two men, but they left behind a journal detailing their time together, and after examining and piecing together its contents – their moments and revelations – logically assuming some missing portions, this is their story as best I can tell it. I have provided direct quotations from the journal where my own words could not match the power of theirs. While the identities of the men will remain anonymous, their story transcends ages. This is a story of peace, in a time of conflict…and these two men are the last remnants of war, for war no longer has a place among humanity.

1

It began midday in the Syrian Desert, when the air was parched and thirsty. The wind from the explosion carried arms, legs, torsos and indiscernible body parts in its whirring dynamo that disintegrated from the heat of the instant fire, leaving only a surreal sprinkling of human ash and torched fragments of military armor that fell the way snowflakes fall, on a frigid, wintry night, but here it was arid and dry and suddenly slow; a lucid, fractured place now wrought with the stench of death. A brief, animate hiss preceded the blast, wreaking instant dread throughout the perimeter. It was a hissing vacuum that drew everything in; the raw suck of life, collecting and sucking in lives and the millions of moments that comprised them, assuming the traits and personality of every soldier. There were no wails or cries. Barely time for final thoughts or telepathic messages of love that often occur upon death. No fore-warnings to duck or dive. There was just an end. Sons, daughters, husbands, wives and best friends were amongst the casualties, but from this blast, not a single corpse would be returning home.

The memories that went with the perished were no doubt of the lasting sort, like they are for any soul, carried into the afterlife like savored, lustrous trophies from life's battle-worn existence and proof of the journey. They were memories of childhood and achievement; first time bike rides, 16th birthdays, first steps, and last; holiday hugs and tender, intimate mornings. These and those unknown were vanquished in one unforeseen interval.

The blast, which occurred just beyond the far western city of Ar Rutbah, was not unforeseen by those who planned it. Were they Sunni or Shiite? Kurds? Were they from Iran or Iraq? Syria or Afghanistan? In the final days of war, perspective became so convoluted that no one really knew who did what. Allegiances shifted like the latest flavor. It all depended on the objective of the moment.

The desert breezes that blew across the lurid, sandy space could not penetrate the cloud of freshly jarred souls. The air hung with grief and the despicable burnt stench of human death. The winds sang a melancholy desert song, one of longing and prescient solemnity – the earth's tribute to the dead. There was the explosion, and then there was nothing, only an unsettling calm. An eerie energy that conveyed the recent occurrence of something murderous and awful, perhaps carrying the spirited orbs of the freshly departed that still hovered in unseen space.

The thick dust, ash and smoke remained for what seemed a few hours, repeatedly colliding and launching off each other, charged by the air and furrowing in weaves; deadened, wasted particles and molecules in the form of body bits and singed hair and skin flakes blending and traversing the landscape. It was a steady rain of DNA.

After perhaps several indistinguishable hours, when it seemed all the world had expired and regurgitated its remains; when all did finally settle, there was movement in the desert sand.

He moved slowly, regaining consciousness with painful effort. Sand stuck to the blood on his face, and parsed and parted when he separated his body from the earth, some of the larger granules permanently embedded in his pores. He was lucky enough to have his limbs intact. He raised his head, forcing his eyes open. He slowly, wearily looked around, trying to see through the smoke. His breathing was heavy. He scanned his body to survey any damage. The patch on his arm was partially torn and frayed, but he could still make it out. He heard a noise and he quickly – instinctually – reached for his handgun that was still on his hip. He drew, pointing his weapon in the direction of the noise that, after a brief but concentrated assessment, sounded like the faint echo of movement in the smoke and open space. He looked upward, but could not see the sky. He looked down, but could barely see the sand. He looked left – nothing. He looked right – nothing, but he continued to hear the rustling of a bag and the jingle of zippers, the sounds of someone unsettled. He kept his gun at the ready and waited, waited for the swirling smoke to break, waited for the zero visibility to improve. While he waited, he recalled what had happened. He remembered his finger on the trigger of his assault rifle. He remembered hearing the hiss and suction of life...he felt it in his soul. The soldiers in his platoon must have felt the same empty pang in their souls. That *knowing* that registers as a dissipating glimmer in the eyes of the soon-to-be-dead. He experienced this *knowing* and his last thought before the blast was one that traveled thousands of miles to America, to his mother and father. And now he found himself wishing he was again a child under his parents, back in that safe, secure bed of no responsibility, under that safe, secure roof, in that safe, secure home that his safe, secure parents had provided. But he was far away from all that.

He was the grandson of a World War II fighter pilot; the son of a decorated Vietnam War veteran, and despite this, his father had urged him not to join, *"Don't do it,"* he now remembered him saying, *"Wars aren't fought the same way anymore. It's not worth it. The glory is gone. The enemies are invisible now – you don't know who they are. It's a different landscape with unfamiliar battles. And this country isn't what it was – you can't trust government anymore. Besides...war is nasty. It's no damn good...no damn good at all."* He replayed these words in his head. He heard his father as if he were standing beside him, and he wished he were...he wished...he wished...in the bleak, uncertain darkness of this fantastic moment...after thousands of days of a colorful life that had led to this one, his wishes were suddenly in black and white.

His mouth was as parched as the desert, and the water he had, in his *Camelbak* pack, evaporated with the blast. He was hesitant to move and reach for his reserve water inside his backpack. When you are alone in a place as big, unending and far stretching as this, the sky becomes your surrogate confidant, and the earth, on whose sand you walk, becomes your inseparable companion. He knew that in the desert the elements are deceptive; they can wear you down, and kill you. A mind ridden with weakness, fear, and conflict will only accelerate the process. Therefore, mental strength was his best ally. It all came down to perception.

He was not sure if his mind was already playing tricks on him, if he had sustained a severe head injury or concussion and did not know it. Was the noise he heard real? Or were they the sounds of the new ghosts of the earth, the hollow sounds of displaced spirits, soldiers still unaware that death had just removed them from this plane? A drip of blood fell to the sand. He stared at the mottled redness of it, unable to recall the last time he saw his own blood. Somewhere on his head was bleeding. He thought the noise seemed closer – someone moving closer to him. He was careful not to shift his body too quickly. The barrel of his gun was fixed on a direction, his finger on the trigger. He could now hear footsteps swishing through the coarse desert sand, still moving... still moving toward him, but he could see nothing except white dust and smoke and swirls of debris, isolated sounds in a virtual whiteout.

Suddenly, the noise ceased, and the figure – the shadowy gray mass that made the noise – stood not six feet from him.

The American soldier slowly rose to his feet. Trickles of blood now ran into his left eye, impeding his vision. All he could see was everything indistinct; dark clothing and the outline of a man. One of the most unnerving aspects of this war was fighting an unknown, unnamed enemy; fighting an *idea* and not a nation.

The two men waited, saying nothing. The smoke continued to slowly clear and move. Myriad thoughts shuttled through the American's head. Slowly, he was able to make out the lower torso and legs of the man opposite him, but still only an outline of the rest. He was hoping it would turn out to be a *friendly* – a fellow comrade.

At least another hour passed, but it was after that hour when the scene became clearer, when the American could finally make out who was across from him.

Just before the blast occurred, the American soldier was face-to-face with a terrorist insurgent. Both had their guns raised and pointed. Both were a second away from pulling the trigger and mortally wounding the other. Just before they could pull their triggers the explosion sent them flying. The two men were on the outer wake of the blast. They had come upon each other in an element of surprise. Both were about to die by the other's bullets – then

BOOM! They were thrown more than thirty yards into the desert sand.

When the smoke cleared, they found themselves face-to-face once again, only this time, they were alone in the desert.

Beads of sweat fast mixed with the sand, blood and desert dust and penetrated the American's head wound while he stood with his gun pointed at the terrorist, his finger on the trigger, once again ready to shoot. Dozens were still alive when this scene last transpired, and as he stood, memories interceded again. He remembered his grandfather's words: *Trust no one – no one! When you're on that battlefield, it's you and only you. Depend on no one!* In his basic training this maxim was invaluable, it worked for him. He quickly earned the reputation for being independent and strong-headed, completing tasks all by himself, even when it was supposed to be the effort of an entire platoon, but he got it done, and garnered the notice of his superiors, who commended his strength and individual discipline. Others soon depended on *him*. He liked it that way, since he possessed the confidence in himself to get it done right, without fail. Failure was one of his biggest fears. It stemmed from grade school when his father would scold him. If he received a "B" on a test, his father asked why he didn't get an "A". If he got two hits out of three at bats in a ball game, his father would ask why he struck out that one time. He didn't resent his father for it, instead he saw it as a challenge to do better. It helped him to always strive for excellence and anything less was at least marginal failure. It also helped groom a strong mind.

When more of the smoke cleared, the American saw that the insurgent had a dislocated shoulder and cuts on his face. His shirt was ripped open revealing his own flow of crimson red blood. He had a rifle in his hands, pointed at the American.

The two men eyed one another. Familiarity seized them, as did a sense of surprise; the irony of staring into the same set of eyes only this time, they held less of a gleam. Thoughts and images traversed through the heads of both men – and at a dizzying pace – scenarios, calculations, situations, assessments and what ifs. As each moment passed, it was another without sound, movement or sign of other life, until they mutually concluded there *was* no other life. It was them…and the desert.

The stand-off continued as dusk approached. There was little movement of body by either man. Sounds of heavy breathing penetrated the tense silence, their breaths combining some-where in the midst; opposing breaths, opposing molecules, gently dispersing the debris-filled air. As time passed, their arms and knees began to shake and acquire numbness from holding the same position. As their arms shook and shivered, so did their guns and their fingers that still remained on the triggers.

The American developed a tick in his neck, each an attempt to jar the sting from his wound. The insurgent began to struggle to hold up his rifle, having lost strength in his shoulder. Beady sweat persisted to roll and traverse down the dusty faces of both men, thick with expression.

In the journal, the American described the showdown:

> *I could not believe I was face to face with this man again. How, I did not know. My clothes were soaked with my own moisture...my body was in pain, but I knew I still had the strength to pull the trigger. And I knew that all patience had already drained from me months ago. I thought of my God, and I wondered how much he really thought of his – if it was as much as most Muslims claim. Was his Allah the same as my God? After all, we are both human.*

Night fell fast, creeping in from nowhere, and the sand acquired a coolness that felt raw against bare skin. This could have been the day when all of the earth – all of nature and its elements – were sent forth from the bowels of hell, for it emitted a strange and alien mystique, mixing and melding with the presence of death and the thousands of years of history nestled in the granules of sand; the histories of war and dissent, nomadic tribes and religious sects, oil and the famed Arabian horses. Where these two men were was not far from time's beginning, and yet, at this moment, both could feel nothing but the imminence of time's end, and the pale turning of doom.

The insurgent smarted in pain. The American continued to squint from the sting of his wound, compounded by the desert dust, the day's debris, and salt, which were ever-present pests in the polluted landscape. Dried mucous filled the orifices of both men, through which the fragile breaths and airs of life came and went. They continued to stare at each other with bitter detest and resentment, unsure of what to do.

The insurgent wrote:

> *I was staring into my own end – my own potential ending, unable to feel the lids on my tired eyes. I now know the thoughts that will choose to bounce through my head upon death, yes of Allah, but also of what might await me. I was prepared for the sand beneath my feet to become my coffin, so to blend back with the earth, but I was also prepared to make the sand beneath the American's feet his own...if I had to. Still, I could not ignore the strange quiet that surrounded me – as if engulfing me. Perhaps this was what slow death felt like.*

The men stared and studied, until trickery became their eyes, and they began to see odd shapes forming in the darkening night, of odd figures and shadowy ogres, both men keenly aware of every passing moment, their lives teetering on each one. Staring and staring, arms gradually falling, sharp pain streaking through limbs...

"Fuck you!" said the American."I said, 'Fuck you,' you're nothing but evil! Another evil Muslim. You gonna pull that trigger or not? C'mon!"

"Kol Khara!"

"What'd you say? *WHAT'D YOU SAY* –"

"Boos teezee!"

The American took a small, jittery step forward. The terrorist insurgent raised his gun, letting out a grunt of pain.

"Yeah, how's that pain feel, you hateful fuck? You'd love to have my head on a platter with an apple in my mouth, wouldn't you? Like you do to the sons of families who don't support you. Like you do to Christians and women. I'm gonna blow you away the same way one of your comrades just did to my men, then *this* American will be the last one standing! You're one Muslim who's not going to take over the world –"

"Ayreh Feek!"

"What are you saying? I know you can speak English, you asshole –"

"I said, 'Fuck you'," said the insurgent, "and before that I said, 'Kiss my ass!'" He finished with a spat of mucous that fell on the American's boot.

The American, with a renewed charge, raised his gun back up and took another step forward. The pace of his breathing increased. His teeth gritted and bloody sweat creased his brow line.

"Go ahead you American fool. Shoot me. What will you gain? It is only you and I here. Or are you too *stupid* to notice?" said the insurgent with Middle Eastern flavor.

The American shook his head, "The world will gain one less evil Muslim!"

"And *then* what will you do? Cry mercy and hope for someone to rescue you?"

"As soon as I turn my back you'll plug me. I know how you Arabs are. You just don't want to die, you coward."

"So let us stay here and rot," said the insurgent. "Let us watch each other decay –"

"You're already rotten. You're already decayed from the inside out. What your people have done – what *you* do! Preying on innocent people, hiding amongst civilians, killing them and their children, raping school children, stoning young girls and women...you have no heart. You only know how to kill and be a coward. You've got that down real well –"

"AND WHAT ABOUT YOU! Your people – you pompous, ignorant Americans, trying to spread your western ways everywhere. You should not be in Arab lands. You do not belong here! We do not want to be like you! You are all hypocrites!"

"*We're* hypocrites? Shut the fuck up!"

"Ah! Is that all you can say, dumb Christian American? *Dumb American!* You Americans are dumb! All those years you fought against communism and now your country is slowly falling under the same doctrine. Look at the rules –"

"Shut up."

"Look at the rules and restrictions on your people! Look how they handicap you with high taxes – pay or go to jail. Pay for your freedom or go to jail. Pay for whatever your government wants to do or go to jail. What democracy is that? It is no longer a nation of the people. Your government controls you and you are too stupid to know it. Look at all their interventions and bailouts. Your country is collapsing! You fight rogue people as you call us, but it is we who have been here for thousands of years, not you. What does it say for your country – your *United States*," he said mockingly, "when two and three year-olds, those who are your future, are already on anti-depressants because the parents of your nation are no longer able to be parents, and one in four of your teenage children need behavior medicine? Is your country really so grand when your children and society are suddenly so imperfect? Your nation is a pinpoint, a single degree away from chaos, from the same chaos, from the same incivility that you so criticize and scrutinize other nations! You think I do not know –"

"Shut up you crazy bastard! At least I have freedom and I'll gladly pay for it! And take ownership for what you started. America hasn't been the same since 9/11, and it won't ever be and I know how that makes you so happy to hear that. The pressures have increased because the laws made to fight you – *you* – are crowding our lives –"

"You tell yourself that. America is greedy. Americans are status driven and materialized. You dig your own grave. You make your own pressures. One day soon you shall learn! The nation of Islam is at your back door. You shall see, just like we are taking over Europe. Our stamp is already on you!"

"No…it's not on me you whacky son of a bitch!" said the American.

"You're no different –"

"I don't want to hear you anymore –"

"No different! Foolish American who cannot see beyond his own nose!"

"Maybe so…but at least I'm not cold enough or foolish enough to kill my own…you have no respect for anything –"

"Innocent people must die for a greater cause! And my brethren know they are exalted by Allah! By the words of the great book –"

"*Exalted*? You mean how they get to screw all those virgins when they die? You're all delusional. You don't even know how to read your own Koran –"

"Allah is great! The Koran is great! You are not even worthy to say the name of my book –"

"You misinterpret and change and manipulate the words of *your book*, to accommodate your own quest for violence and dominance! Muhammed never slayed anyone when he returned to Mecca! You have made the Koran a book of hate and destruction! You call *us* hypocrites? Islam forbids its people from desecrating the bodies of the dead, and what do you do? So shove your corrupted Koran up your soiled ass along with the bullets from my gun –"

"You are the infidel! Infidel!" said the ISIS soldier, his voice creaking. "YOU ARE THE INFIDEL! YOU SOIL THESE LANDS WITH YOUR WAYS AND THE VERY BREATH FROM YOUR MOUTH! YOU ARE IN NO PLACE TO COMMENT ON MY KORAN! YOU –"

"BUT YOU ALL COME OVER AND ENJOY *OUR WAYS*! Is that it? Huh?" said the American, who took two lunging steps forward and forcibly shoved the ISIS soldier back. It sent the insurgent staggering. He was surprised by the American's move, even as they stood gun to gun. "You hate us but you enjoy our freedom," the American continued. "It's okay for you to pollute our lands with your heretical Muslim ways? Is it? Is it! We're not telling you to change your religion, but you come to America and expect us to change ours – to *adopt* yours! America was founded on Christian principles, and you can't change that, you son of a bitch, because *that's* our history! Now open your mouth so I can cleanse your filthy body with my pure American bullets…OPEN IT!"

For the first time the terrorist responded with silence, slowly lowering his arms…and his gun, before opening his mouth. The American rested the barrel of his gun on the Muslim's lower lip. The Muslim started to shiver and his eyes started to fill with water. The American stared at his target, defiance crinkling his face and nose, but the sound of bullets did not come, and when the Muslim saw that the American could not pull the trigger, he slowly backed away and closed his mouth. Solemnity welled in the ISIS soldier's eyes and registered on his face. "We are under the same sky," the Muslim said at last, his words coming out slowly, deliberately, "we are both cloaked in the same material called skin. You say you do not kill your own, but what do you wish to do now?"

"I'm not one of you. Don't try to manipulate *me*. Don't even *try* to twist this around and go there –"

"Do it. Pull your trigger then. Avenge those dear to you who lost their lives on 9/11, who lost their lives here in this desert and throughout the Middle East. Avenge your fellow soldiers and comrades. I'm not afraid of you. Only remember...9/11 is every day in these parts. Loss here is a daily occurrence –"

"And you weren't going to kill me? You hate America out of resentment because what you experience is *not* a daily occurrence in the United States. Because you suffer misery, is it fair to want to spread your misery to others? I should have sympathy for you? Americans believe in life. Heretical Muslims, your actions show, relish death! What sanctity is that? Don't you get it? Every time you kill somebody you subtract from the entire human race – you don't *add* to it." The American spoke calmly, evenly, his gun still ready to fire, his muscles taut and resolved.

"Oh, I see, and you don't kill *anyone*. Do you hear yourself? You are a clueless American. The American institutions believe in life? Really? But they put chemicals in their food and elsewhere, approved by your government, and they peddle addictive pharmaceuticals. Yes...I *did* want to kill you, but I am *not* a fool. I may not like you...but I now see that we may need each other. And you can say whatever you want, but I realize that we are all we have at this moment...and besides, where are we in this war? Not just me and you, but our nations? What has this brought us to? It has helped hasten the world to a crossroads – a battle of power. Every world leader standing on the curb of their own nation shouting at one another...like you and I are shouting. I see we are behaving no different."

"And I'm supposed to trust *you*? I'm actually fucking reasoning with you? Maybe you're just acting like this because you're all alone," said the American. "Or are you just too scared to die?"

The American wondered, to what nation did this terrorist claim to belong? He was having difficulty discerning the moment – sifting it into parts. There was that body of knowledge that he knew. He *knew* from experience the mentality of the terrorists and insurgents he fought. He *knew* from the battle fatigue he felt; from lugging eighty pounds on his back from place to place, going sixteen to eighteen hours a day, and weeks without a shower or hot meal. He *knew* from the RPG's, EFP's and IED's, from the snipers and mortars and drive bys; from constantly having to have eyes behind his head and unable to stay in any one place too long, always needing to know the whereabouts of the closest cover; he *knew* from having to reload so many times. He *knew* from the weariness that was his...and the sleep that was lost. He *knew* from the hours of silent, thoughtful prayer, and the deep thoughts that became a prayer. He *knew*...he *knew* he shouldn't negotiate with terrorists – not ever, not because of policy, but because of who they are; their own determined resolve and cold, hardened hearts. He *knew* the terrorist insurgents did not care about Iraq, or Syria or Egypt or Afghanistan, and Libya, and that they were hurting the people and the progress of the countries. He did not know what they cared about – except for dying...dying without regret for having done something more worthwhile with their lives. However, he also *knew* that governments had so much to do with it, and that their policies forced the people of many nations to become harsh, critical judges of others.

The two men again stared at each other, looking into each other's eyes, searching, thinking, minds spinning. The American's gun was still raised. "And later, when we don't need each other you'll want to kill me again," said the American.

"If you put a bullet in me now, 'later' won't matter. Will it? I will tell you this...that now nor later will I ever disgrace and mock your holy book as you have mine."

"Oh, so that's where all this feely bullshit is coming from...because I told you to shove your Koran up your dirty ass..."

"My ass is no more dirty than you, your mouth, your very being; our entire wretched humanity. My Koran is just as precious to me as your Bible is to you –"

"That's all melancholy bullshit. Maybe you should have taught philosophy or religion instead of joining ISIS or whoever the fuck you are, and targeting innocent people –"

"I did. I taught at the university."

The American paused. "Well…y-you should have stayed. You *are* fucking crazy."

"Are you trying to give me a compliment, Mr. American Christian Soldier? I should be honored that I am showered with these words from you, who is so superior to I…"

"Fuck you. Don't patronize me. I value and save lives…you kill and die selfishly for your own twisted ideology. I'm not going to fall for your pitiful bullshit. No way…no fucking way."

The argument continued to froth, a steady volley of nerves and spite. Their argument… their disagreement and points of contention were in fact microcosms of war; seeds from which sprout the movement of guns, tanks, ammunition, fuel, bombs, nukes, soldiers – roots of death. Hate, bullets and bombs bestowed upon the earth, beneath the picturesque sky, seemed so wrong and cynical, so surreal and the hyper-reality of existence; earth's purity versus mankind's destructive and wretched savagery. If life was like the sky – if people were like the blue of the sky, there would never have been war.

An argument is a form of war like a disagreement between neighbors that escalates into a fistfight. Is it really much different than a disagreement between nations that are moved to battle? What might this say about the human species and about ourselves? It is my belief, as humanity has begun to discover, that if we pause and go within for our peace, to realize our own innate empowerment, and to channel and use the love we have for others as our power and guide, then peace is indeed possible, and an easier practice than any argument ever was. Harmony and positivity can spread faster than a virus or any form of negativity; harmony and positivity are far more powerful than negativity has ever been. When harmony spreads, a resonant frequency is born.

Solitude and harmony are worthy beliefs and aspirations of a people, but in the time of these two men, both were elusive on a mass scale. The existent reality needed to be challenged and a new one forged. This American and this insurgent, unbeknownst to both, were embroiled in the rehash of a reality that was already past them, but bitterness has a way of seething like a gathering storm or a nagging pestilence; bitterness is a poison that can be so severe it can result in disease. Both men were slowly facing a moment of admission that seemed too fantastic to grasp, because something was happening that was vastly unexpected. A new war had hatched – the inner war of wills – one abutting another; a common show of overly proud men that, in the course of human history, has had extreme results, none of it ever good, demonstrating the oft ill-fate of ego.

And so it was that the two men resumed their stand-off, heavy with diatribes and insults, cutting remarks intended to do the job of bullets; piercing or ending the perceptible order of differences, and that's just what it was – just what was being verbally unleashed, a distinct order of issues not only with each other, but directed toward a whole nation or a whole group, its government and its people; a neat, unflappable order of differences, at times a lashing tirade with no sensible sequence, voiced while the bullets remained inside their respective guns, at least to this point, albeit locked, loaded and ready.

After long exchanges in the looming desert-darkness, silence would intercede and control their stand-off before something else would heave off the chest of either man, a release of another ounce of difference. It was evident that the stand-off *had to* resume; it was necessary in order to bring about a reversal of their dissent, but first they had to determine if the reversal was even possible.

"You come here and wreak havoc with our way of life –" said the ISIS soldier.

"What! *Your* way of life? *What* way of life? What way of life do you have –"

"Oh, the American ignorance –"

"You teach your children to hate and kill!" And before the Muslim could utter another word, anticipating each attempt, the American with his gun still pointed and ready to fire, screamed, "HATE AND KILL...! HATE AND KILL...! HATE AND KILL! KILL! KILL! Yeah...where is your sorrow now, you weasel? A little while ago you're crying over your Ko-ran! Now what? Fuck this and fuck you! You tell me about your state of affairs, Mr. *Professor*...you rant and rave. You act as though we Americans don't know what's going on – maybe some don't, but many do. That's why we rally whenever tragedy strikes, because we all know what was lost. We love our freedom. We enjoy our money when we have it, and we can vote people in or out of office, and that's called *democracy*, you son of a bitch. And it's true, America isn't what it was. Not anymore. You think I don't know that? But at least we still honor our dead soldiers. Every single one. What funerals do you have? Do you go out and retrieve all of your dead fellow ISIS warriors? I haven't seen it yet. I *have* seen them gunned down in bunches, only to be left there in the street to rot. What honor do you have? You call it honor to celebrate a suicide bomber before he goes out and kills countless numbers of un-armed, innocent, peace-wanting, life-loving civilians! Only to say you did it for Allah! *Allah?* You've got to me kidding me. God. Allah. Tell me what the real difference is. Tell me… would your Allah *really* advocate the spread of violence and senseless death? Would He really advocate and support jetliners flying into buildings and bringing them down? Would any God? The very notion is a contradiction. Your actions are an insult to His name!"

The Muslim insurgent was silent for a time, thinking and constructing a reply. "I find your reply interesting," he said at last, "I must ask… *who* are you fighting for? Who do you *think* you are fighting for if your country is not what it once was?"

"Look…I'm not going to philosophize with you," said the American, "we're either going to blow each other away or not…"

"Or you could just blow me away…"

"I can now barely fucking see you."

"Well, that might be fun…but what then? You'd be alone in this big desert."

"When I could be alone with you? I don't believe this." The American stared as hard as he could, shifted his feet in the sand, and lowered his weapon. "Look…I'm fucking tired. I got blood, sweat…and all kinds of shit in my eyes. I know why I fight – in my mind I fight for the commoner. I fight for freedom and its preservation in America. I fight for my friends sitting on a couch with their family watching a ball game. I fight for peace and democracy in your

Middle fucking East! And I fight for these kids out here, who run around without shoes, starving, begging and desperate, who can still smile, who *want* what we're trying to give them, and whose hearts aren't yet turned. As for governments and people in power...right now I'm not fond of either, but I honor my duty. I just wish the anti-war protesters would instead have silent, pro-peace rallies, *and then* maybe they would have better results. You keep damn protesting war and more just keeps coming. It's where the focus is. But I *do* believe in fighting to protect a nation's sovereignty –"

"You swear an awful lot."

"What the fuck – and you swear in Arabic, what's the difference? You may be a teacher but you're not fucking mine so shut up, and besides –"

"What is your occupation in America? Or are you a full-time soldier?"

"What...? This isn't a meet and greet hour. What the fuck with the questions! Are we on a game show? You're a goddamn terrorist and I have a gun in my hand!"

"There is one in mine too, Mr. American."

The American exhaled a tired, exasperated breath and lowered his arms *completely* by his side, the handgun now *hanging* from his hand, but he did not remove his eyes from the ISIS soldier. "You make one fast move and I'm blowing you away," he said. He winced when he gently touched the wound on his head that had stopped bleeding, having coagulated with the help of the debris in the desert air, the salt of his sweat, the afternoon heat...and his decreasing blood pressure.

The men's watch on one another continued. A soft, night breeze swept through them, and the terse desert silence ushered in an accord of the most fragile sorts.

The ISIS soldier wrote:

> *Perhaps it was the desert night and exhaustion that overcame us. I am not quite sure what it was. Both our words were wounding, and I realized how much more painful they can be*

than bullets. If I was asked to summarize or re-peat the words I spoke to him...I am not sure that I would be able. They were spoken in a frenzy. Does this admission take worth from the words? I do not know. But when our guns fell to our sides, I did know that we were in-stantly thrust into the most unlikely of fates.

The unknown still lingered. Neither knew what was left of the other side. During the hours that they had traded barbs in the desert sand, not a single plane, jet, helicopter or drone was seen or heard overhead. While they fired insult after insult, not a single voice was heard, besides their own. No lights could be seen. No campfire. No oil lamp. No camel, horse or ani-mal. No other movement – at all, anywhere, for as far as their eyes could see. All they *could* see was each other.

"I'm thinking...should we dig in and sleep here?" said the ISIS soldier.

"It's too soon for that."

"I'm not asking you to sleep with me."

"That's not what I meant, asshole. Don't start!" said the American with a glare.

Slowly, hesitantly, each with a heavy study of the other, they turned and began walking, the American with a backpack strapped to his back and the ISIS soldier a large satchel draping his one healthy shoulder. It was a mutual understanding of choice that roused their movement; completely unaware where their sudden and new journey would take them – completely unaware of the impact it would have on their lives, as well as the lives of future generations. The only awareness that was present when they began trekking on that dark, azure night, leaving behind death and the hair-raising feel of hovering spirits, was of themselves. After reading the journal entries from this time, I sensed that both men felt as if they were quite possibly the last two humans alive in the world – in the very least, *this part* of the world. They had no idea how close to the truth that sensation actually was. History and humankind were in the course of a cataclysmic change; a chasm in the former continuity of humanity, and they were walking through it...or perhaps, it could later be said, that they were walking *to it*.

2

They walked for an extended duration without a word between them. Their communication was in a look or sideward glance or eye of scorn. However, this could not last. Curiosity and a burning bitterness were catalysts for further dialogue, albeit colored and underscored by a snide detestation for the other – or rather, the *ways* of the other. But just how deep *did* this detestation run? Would one man's outlast the other?

"Why did you leave your job as a university professor?"

"I was filling in for a friend, hoping that it would lead to a job for me too."

"So it didn't?"

The ISIS soldier was quiet in reply, before finally responding, "I don't want to argue."

"Why would we? Were you about to say something that would cause one?"

"Possibly."

"Say it. I'll try my best."

"That doesn't sound too convincing."

"Too bad…I can't believe I'm even fucking walking beside you –"

"Then you better not get too close."

A silence stuck between them for several long paces, before the ISIS soldier continued the story.

"My friend got killed by an Israeli bullet. Left three children and a wife behind."

"And that was when you took up his cause – or went to fight for it?"

"It was the beginning of things. I went to help, and then one event led to another…yes."

"And that's how you're here with me now."

"Yes."

"That's it?"

"Yes…were you expecting more? Orphaning three children and making a widow is not enough?"

"Hmm…"

"You think I'm lying…"

"I didn't say that. Just sounds too simple. That's all it took for you to join ISIS? Where I come from it seems it should be much more to join a terrorist organization that is bent on murder and bloodbath."

The ISIS soldier did not immediately reply. He could only stare back at the American, searching his eyes that were illuminated by the moonlight. "Maybe there is more."

"Oh, yeah…I was an EMT," said the American, breaking another spell of silence.

"You what?"

"You asked before what I did back in America…I was an EMT. An Emergency Medical –"

"I know what it is. My sister lives in America and I lived there for a short while."

"Now see, I could take issue with that and argue…but I won't. All's I'll say is that many of your terrorist brothers and sisters usually *enjoy* our land and its freedoms, *and then* you try to blow us up."

"Well –"

"No. Leave it alone. Just shut up and leave it at that. You said you didn't want to argue."

"Okay."

"Good. Fuck you."

"And fuck you too. What else?"

"I'm an EMT in New York City and I was born in Long Island."

"My sister lives in Bayridge," said the ISIS soldier.

"I used to live in Bayridge. Interesting place. Lots of your kind there," said the American.

"My *kind*...you speak as though we are aliens –"

"Your race of people. Your heritage and culture –"

"I knew what you meant."

"I'll surprise you with this...I used to date a Palestinian woman in Bayridge before I got married."

The ISIS soldier stopped walking, dismay coloring his face.

"Yeah, yeah," said the American. "Let's go, I want to keep moving."

"Wait."

"What?"

"I am also Palestinian...I am from Palestine –"

"Okay...so?" said the American, but the ISIS soldier from Palestine still did not move. "And? Am I supposed to clap for you? I don't have any medals in my pocket to give you." The Palestinian still did not move. "Okay, okay, I get it. C'mon."

"Why do you portray yourself as having such a low tolerance for *my kind* as you say?"

"*Tolerance? Tolerance?* Oh, so I should tolerate cold-blooded, third world murderers who are trained to shoot a gun by age five...and trained to hate, and behead –"

"Okay! So you dated a Palestinian –"

"Yeah, but am I still with her? Now let's keep moving."

"Are you?"

"I told you I got married."

"So...Americans seem to have a problem of cheating on each other. They always want better and suffer from the illusion that it is out there."

"What? Some of the shit you say – no, I don't do that. I'm not that guy. Now watch your mouth and let's fucking go! Besides, there are whores in the lands of Arabia too!"

The American later told the Palestinian that in civilian society he lived by three rules: *Trust no one except yourself, your mother and your father. Never get involved with a married woman, and never try and save anyone from themselves – from the life that they created – because you can't save them no matter how hard you try. They'll just keep on living that life...it's who they are...it's what they know. Try and save them for too long and you destroy yourself too.*

"I did not intend to anger you," said the Palestinian, resuming his pace.

"Look," said the American, pointing his finger at the Palestinian, "you're still my enemy, so don't think you're getting all fucking nice with me."

Another word did not pass between them until daybreak, when the hot sun slowly rose out from the bed sheets of the earth, quickly dispersing the small pockets of cool desert air. The heat reminded both men of charred remains. It was a sweltering, blistering sun. A baking sun. To the American it felt like he was being slowly cooked and singed, far removed from hot dogs and popcorn at a ballpark for a summer game. To the Palestinian, it was like his skin was without moisture, and he said a silent, inner prayer for refuge – for both he *and* the American.

For both men, there was a nauseating crustiness to the morning from having trekked all night with blast debris in their hair and the microscopic cell fragments from dead comrades scattered about their clothes and skin, but they continued to walk through the desert, it was all they *could* do; that big, vast space of earth, brown and tan with stubble, like walking

across the face of creation, with sprouts of or-
phaned vegetation and idle bushes – the desert
misfits of their species – and withered trees
that had started but could not keep, surrender-
ing their short lives to the sun. It was not the
most palatable of places, but it was peaceful,
and far away from any world or situation that
either man had known – even for the Palestinian. In the middle of the desert his burdens
were not with him; they were not there lurking
in the rough sand over which he passed. No
immediate family worries or pressures, no
causes to vanquish, and I wonder if he thought
or had a sense that his days of fighting were indeed over. For the American…there were no
bills to pay or letters to write or orders to follow. No officers to protect. Thoughts of home
intruded his troubled mind, but he was also
feeling something invasive in his heart, something with which he was not quite ready to
share space; he too must have felt the peace
that exuded from the desert under that morn-
ing-coated sky, and he had to wrestle with the

reconciliation of it, since it countered everything else that was boiling within him.

The American wrote:

> *Out here is different. Something is different and everything is different all at once. It is an odd sensation to be alone in a place as large as this, and hard to put into words. There's no one else around! The best way I can put it is this: Out here it's like some eternal lull, like the earth has paused to watch only us. It feels like a detoxification from life, the life I've always known, but was never sure of or never quite certain I was in the place I should be. Out here I don't feel that concern and under the circumstances – who I'm with – I've had trouble accepting that notion, as if my soul is in a state of suspension. But these moments are all I have now. All I can do is trek forward.*

They walked…these two men with the earth, into the wide future, lured there, desert step by desert step.

"May I ask," said the Palestinian at last, "why did you break up with the Palestinian woman in Bayridge?"

"You're still on that one, are you? You been thinking about that all night?"

"Maybe. If you don't want to talk about it we don't have to –"

"Why did you join ISIS?"

"It's a long story."

"Well, we're in the middle of a long desert going somewhere that still looks like nowhere to me –"

"We should be heading towards Syria – or Jordan, and in the direction of Israel."

"Hmm…my compass is smashed so I hope you're right."

"And what if I'm wrong? Where will we end up?" said the Palestinian.

"For me, maybe in hell, surrounded by a bunch of heretical Muslims. How else do you expect me to answer that? Maybe we'll end up in a Coney Island wiener joint, or *somefucking*-where…"

"Or nowhere, and maybe we'll be left eating our hands."

"Whatever…it's a long, hot day ahead, so I think I have time for your long story."

"I'll answer you if you answer me."

"What? What is it with you? Did you skip pre-school? What are we 10 years old?"

"Now who has all the questions –"

"Fuck you. You sound like a little –"

"I wish we were. Maybe we wouldn't be enemies or at war."

"Oh, really? Little kids don't fight?" said the American with a steady glare upon his adversary.

They *had* been conversing, conversing unlike enemies, much to the American's dismay, who was grappling with the actuality of it; grappling with his own apprehension and war-filled, country-prided spite, but the ISIS soldier's statement was a reminder, and it compelled the American to check his holster and formulate how best to proceed if he needed to draw.

"So you still intend to use that on me?"

"Yours is still around your shoulder too..." said the American.

"Sly, sly American."

"Don't mock me. It's still early in the morning. You want to start this now?"

"I'm not the one who checked my gun."

"That's because I'm trained to be wiser than you."

"Oh! Ohhh!" exclaimed the Palestinian, stopping in the sand. "Oh! The American pomposity finally –"

It spurred the American to burst into laughter – a deep, instinctual, hearty, bellowing laughter that he could not suppress, born deep from the joviality that once possessed him.

"You laugh! You think it's funny – you... you...you think...," but the Palestinian could not finish his sentence. The American's laughter overwhelmed his every attempt. It was a boisterous and buoyant laugh – healthy in every way, and the thing about laughter, is it reaps more laughter. It is a human phenomenon that laughter can be so contagious. Since it is not done enough, few ever realize that it is a contagion. Even the most maddening of humans will eventually crack a smile and surrender to incessant laughter. And so it was that the Palestinian was no different, for he too could not help but start laughing, and in frustration the Palestinian could only muster, "You...you...! You stink!" And soon after, it was a scene that skeptics and scholars would not have believed. Perhaps it could be blamed on desert delirium and fast-rising temperatures from the maturing sun, but I'd like to believe it was the result of human emotion in its purest form and its amazing power, the commonalities of humanity, a bridge of mutual human capacity; a welcome, contagious release after witnessing nothing but war and horror. Here was the scene: An American soldier and an ISIS terrorist from Palestine alone in the desert, laughing hysterically, laughing loudly, their faces red not from the sun, but from laughter, and after a time fueling each other's laughter.

It was a cultural oxymoron. I cannot help but think that some of the laughter was eventually fueled by the incredible and bizarre occurrence itself; that both men found it equally hysterical to be mutually immersed in a fancied fit of gaiety that rumbled throughout their entire bodies.

By the time their laughter reached a cessation, they were both sitting on the desert sand after having doubled over and fallen there.

In the journal the Palestinian wrote:

> *I found myself face-to-face with this American, on the sands of Syria. His face was red and I could feel the redness of my own. His mouth was still smiling, and I could still feel the upturn of my own. This American – this Christian – who I am supposed to hate, but in this candid moment it was not hate that I felt, but rather a union between two humans experiencing a moment of humanity.*

"While we're sitting, we better get some strength and have breakfast," said the American. "I have an MRE of scrambled eggs and sausage...," and before the Palestinian could answer, "...if you don't mind sharing – it's best to conserve –"

"You better be careful going against your will like this and being nice, it might become a habit."

"Do you want some or not, wiseass?"

"Of course – yes, thank you. Thank you. I would be happy to share."

The American opened his backpack and took out the MRE along with a canteen of water that was no doubt already warm from the heat of the desert.

"In my culture, in ancient times," said the Palestinian, "what you are doing with your food is very honorable. You are giving me your *sop*, we used to call it, and some still do – you are giving to me of the choicest bite of your food. It is done with special respect and... and...good will," he finished softly, the softness of his final words barely audible.

"Well then," said the American, after mixing water with the ready-to-eat meal, "go ahead and take the first bite from my sop."

"No…let this bite be your sop. The first bite on this morning, our first breakfast…this is the best bite, and the tastiest. And it makes you a most generous host."

The two men shared the rest of the meal in silence, passing it back and forth, alternating mouthfuls. After it was finished, they reclined in the sand, nursed their wounds and let their tired bodies rejuvenate.

"When I was a boy," said the Palestinian, "we ate raw grain. It was a bonding ritual to stop in a field and rub ears of grain and laugh and talk with a friend or family member, and then eat it under this same warm sun. I can remember always walking home feeling freshness on my face, as if I had just partied with the earth. On other days I would press grapes and get silly, not knowing at the time that my silliness was my novice drunkenness… with grape juice stains on my feet and coloring my skin and clothes. I would smell the smells of old wine all of over my body for a whole week, but it was such a good smell – the sniff of nature…"

The American held his gaze out across the desert, entranced there, his wispy thoughts many miles and days and memories beyond.

"Well," said the Palestinian, noticing the American's absence, "we should cover up and get moving before the sun has peaked in the sky, or we'll bake just like that grain I ate that could barely sway under the weight of the sun."

About this time the Palestinian wrote:

> *The American has kindness. He reminded me of my days in the fields of Palestine. Under his brute strength I did feel a bond of humaneness, one that I was not yet used to, but it was there. Despite my lack of assurance in him, this was a moment, one that gave welcome refuge to my heart and restored some prospect that I may still yet have faith in man. One other thing*

*about the American...he hasn't any fear –
none. He is a strong, robust Christian soldier,
inside and out.*

They no sooner started to walk again when the Palestinian winced in pain.

The American stopped. "Wait a minute," he said. "Your shoulder is dislocated. Why don't you let me try to pop it back into place?"

The Palestinian studied the American's face, studied his eyes and the size of the squint in them. He studied and weighed...

"Alright forget it," said the American, "let's just keep walking –"

"Okay I will let you. You know what you're doing?"

"I'm an EMT –"

"I know that. There are bad EMT's you know!"

"I can't make it any worse, now stop whining."

"You could break it."

"That's true. I can also throw a 90 mile per hour fastball. I guess you'll have to trust me."

"What do fastballs have to do with this? Do you plan on throwing one at me?"

"You got a baseball?" The American smirked. "The weather reminds me…that's all."

"You used to play?"

"Yeah, and I still do. Hold still. Try and relax. Grab my waist for leverage. We need to stabilize it. Let's hope the swelling around the joint isn't bad."

The American worked on the Palestinian's shoulder until it was back in place and proportionate to the rest of his body, instead of hanging limp and useless. He made a makeshift sling and put it on the Palestinian, before they resumed walking.

"So you want to know why I broke up with the Palestinian girl?"

"You have a knack for remembering my questions, even the ones you do not wish to answer," said the Palestinian.

"You asked it. I'll answer it."

"Okay."

"There were differences," started the American, and of course there had to be, as his mind traveled thousands of miles back to New York City. There he was in Bayridge, Brooklyn. He could see her face again, it's what memories do, they summon the intricacies of a past, bringing forward the roseated details that were once strong enough or pleasant enough to be permanently nested in the mind. Memories are reminders that we're not just human, but time machines capable of returning to moments that we've already lived, if but exclusively through the senses. He recalled the shape of her lips, because he liked her stout, pillowy lips and how they were thick enough to envelop his own. He recalled her soft smile because he remembered how it would soften his mood. He loved seeing her walk in after her jog through the city, how she looked, it moved him, with her flushed face, healthy bangs of hair falling over her eyes, and sweat on her forehead; her sweat building in the crevice of the small of her back. He could recall many lovemaking sessions following those jogs, and again after she got out of the shower. In the desert, the smell of her skin filled his senses all over again. Because of her asthma she could only jog in the warm months, so, for a gift, he bought her a treadmill. They would both look forward to Saturday mornings, when they would sleep in, lounge and nestle in each other's arms, and stay in bed until close to noon, lying amidst light talk and the beautiful silence of fulfillment and contentment, save for a gasp or sigh as they traded light massages or soft tickles up and down each other's arms that sent tingles everywhere. This would happen before getting up and sharing morning coffee, just them with the morning, with sunshine flitting through the blinds and some light jazz playing in the background – usually Coltrane or Monk or Miles Davis. He then recalled their arguments and how they were always based on differences in culture, not in human reason, but at the time he perceived them as faulty reasoning – *her* fault, not his. Now older, he knew that his initial assumption was set in ignorance, for empathy now told him that she spoke and opined from what she knew, and what she had known was a result of culture – his being vastly different from hers. A part of him wished he was wiser when he was younger…that he had gotten to know her for who she was, and he only came to this conclusion because of what would befall him later. He remembered she always wanted to keep trying, but he let go. He let that languid indifference and resignation that begins any separation to commence his detachment, and in the desert, remembering it all, he beat himself up once again.

"What kind of differences?" asked the Palestinian.

The American looked across at the Palestinian with an expression that said everything – that said, *Why are you asking what you already know?* Before turning to look out across the expanse of the desert landscape, organizing his thoughts, measuring his words…

"9/11 differences. I'm native to New York *and* to America, so it affected me differently than it did her. I was with her when it happened."

"You were mad that she did not sympathize with you?" said the Palestinian.

"Do you know what it feels like to have concrete and steel floors fall down on your little head and squeeze your brain's matter through your ears while your last thoughts are of your wife and kids, and how you don't know why the fuck you're dying? Then POOF! Your entire body and being is disintegrated into dust and your soul is jolted into the abyss without warning? Do you?"

The Palestinian was silent and did not immediately answer.

"I'm asking you in seriousness. I'm not trying to argue," said the American.

"I have seen much death. Senseless, irrational death. I have had men die in my arms and seen children mutilated before me. I have tried to imagine what they felt before death. I have tried –"

The Palestinian had grown accustomed to tears, ever since he was a boy, when he bore witness to the bloody death of an uncle who strayed obliviously into the line of fire, on the street in front of his home. He died with a smile on his face, smiling right at him, waving to him as he departed. A smile full of life and love, and then he was gone.

"But have you tried to carry that beyond your own people? Did you wonder what it felt like for the victims of all these bombings, and what it felt like for their families? The pain?"

"I could pose the same question to you."

"But this is a question you asked me – about the Palestinian woman."

"I *have* tried."

"And?"

"I do what you do – what you have done."

The American responded with a look of suspicion.

"I put it out of my mind as soon as it comes in," said the Palestinian.

The American kept walking. What the Palestinian spoke was truth. Soldiers cannot fight a war with empathy for *both* sides. Especially their war, with all of the complexities it had, being shot at or encountering an IED planted by virtually anyone representing one of the many sides in the conflict. Thus, there *must* only be enough empathy for *one* side – your own. It is one of the natures of war – one of the myriad facts of war.

"You do not have a reply, Mr. American."

"Yeah, so?"

"I do what I must, just as you do –"

"But those people –"

"– were civilians, yes!" said the Palestinian, stopping in the sand. "I *have* thought of them. Is that not enough? War is awful. And I will tell you this, I've been fighting it not only against you, who we label the infidels, but also in my very home. All of *life* is a war! Every damn moment! Is it not?"

The question resonated with the American, who acknowledged it with silence.

"I have been fighting shame!" the Palestinian continued, "I have been fighting the whispers that penetrate my mind. You do not know, Mr. Christian American! I bet you did grow up on a nice street, in a nice house –"

"And you hate me for it! Just like everybody else who's in these lands and over the age of twenty –"

"No! I envy you for it! ENVY! You have known a comfort that I will never, ever know! You have walked out of your house to a tree-lined street, without guilt, without threat, and without fear of a bomb falling on your head! You have known the comfort of peace on a bedtime pillow. I have not –"

"Why envy us? Why? When we have tried to give it all to you and lead by example –"

"I am not yet finished! Why must we change our lives and way of living? Why must we change centuries of habit and ritual? Why? Why can we not have the same peace that you have known, but within the boundaries of my existent culture? In my own land? And I will tell you this, Mr. American –"

"Stop fucking patronizing me or I'll drop you right here!" said the American, pointing his finger.

"Fine...but I will tell you this. *My* fellow Muslims – my fellow comrades, would never have admitted to thinking about those dead Americans on 9/11 –"

"Then maybe it's a good thing you did admit it," said the American, snapping his head forward and resuming his walk through the sand.

"Why? Why do you say that?" said the Palestinian, but the American kept walking. "I want to know why!" The Palestinian screamed after him.

The American, already several paces ahead, suddenly stopped and turned. "Because that's how close you were to being dead. It's how close both of us are to being dead by our own bullets. Don't you see that? We've had *two* prime opportunities to blow each other away, and maybe, just maybe, that's why it's just you and me in this desert right now. Because you *did* admit it. Because just maybe both of us are that much different than all the rest. I broke up with the Palestinian woman because we argued about this. I was infuriated. I couldn't see past that anger, and she couldn't see into it. I felt for those people in the towers, and I loved one of them. My cousin was in there." The American's head lowered in dejection. "But I also loved *her*..."

The American turned and started walking again. The Palestinian, in a half-jog, caught up.

"I understand you. What you felt and what you feel is your right. I understand you. Do you hear me? I do see past your anger because I have it to. Do you understand what I am saying? Do you?"

The American kept walking, his eyes downward, staring at the hot sand.

Suddenly, the Palestinian grabbed the American by the arm, spun him around and stopped him. The American's surprise registered on his face, but he did not reach for his gun.

"Do you understand what I am saying? This part of you I know. Do you understand this?" asked the Palestinian.

"Yes...," said the American.

The Palestinian released his grip and the two men stood facing one another under the blazing sun.

"What was her name?" asked the Palestinian, as they began to walk again.

"*Sanaa*...I called her, *Sanni* –"

"That was my sister's name –"

"Sanni?"

"No...Sanaa...my sister in Bayridge..."

The two men paused.

"Probably different girl though, right?" said the Palestinian, nervous energy coloring his words.

"Yeah...yeah, most definitely," said the American. "Had to have been."

"But she was a brunette," said the Palestinian.

"Yeah, she was a brunette. Shoulder-length," said the American.

"Yes…but many Palestinians are brunettes."

An uncomfortable silence followed, timelines and probability equations running through each of their heads as they walked under an omnipresent sun that continued to slowly bake the earth; baked the desert, where the desert sand without cessation lapped the desert heat. It was a merciless place and a place of mercy all at once, and a place with little natural cover.

"You stopped bleeding," said the Palestinian.

"Yeah. I think it was a piece of hot metal that branded me."

"Same here. I got a piece in the back of my neck."

"Fuck it. I guess the sun scorched it closed…" And it did, the baking heat accelerated the scabbing stage, like a kiln it baked the wound into a scab.

"Yes…*fuck it* – and the blowing sand, it is good for closing open wounds when hot."

The American smirked and nodded, "Yeah…"

At this point in the journey and their journal, I discovered dozens of granules of sand stuck in the binding, some having gotten loose and scattered about the pages. Were they put there? Or did they blow there? There was also a dried leaf from a rare desert flower. I imagine that if one were looking overhead at these two men as they trekked across this enormity of starched earth, they would see two dots amidst an uninterrupted area; a clean and antiseptic space untainted and unsettled by humanity.

The Palestinian wrote:

> *Out here, the barren baseness of an epoch, the beginning of history, like an eldest son, this was Allah's first yawn (or for the American, it was God's). I understood the American. I wondered if we were adequate representatives of our respective sides. Or was it that we all, as humans, possessed a common ground because we possessed common traits; the ability to exercise common feelings and emotions, but it was war and religious indifference – our interpretation of both – and ego, that smothered*

that possibility like the smote of hope? Out here I perceive my land differently. The land I knew that was home – this whole Middle East – is now strangely alien to me, as if I have entered into a different conscience, because of this man with whom I walk, and because we are so alone here. The whole of it is already a mystery to me, like the workings and histories of our souls.

3

There were still no sounds or signs of other life besides their own, anywhere. Nothing was normal and everything was awry, even the air seemed to be in a state of confusion, and these instinctual perceptions extended globally; all of existence within the world and without, was in flux, as if a quantum dimension had intruded from the ether, but the American and the Palestinian had no way of knowing it.

The men soon began encountering a desert terrain that formed waves and steep, imposing hills of sand that could have easily engulfed them if nature had ordered, and perhaps it would have – seizing them in their dark shadows and quickening sand, had it not been perhaps, for the desert's desire to see just how these two men would fare as they continued through the nebulous and contentious triangle of territories that was Iraq, Syria and Jordan, that buffered the most contentious of all lands – Israel.

"I believe it's your turn," said the American.

"Yes."

"Sorry I don't have a lectern for you."

"How gracious of you. I suppose the sand dunes will do. You know…I had a student from America – a very pretty female student, who had affections for me. She would –"

"Wait a minute. 'Affections'? You mean she wanted to sleep with you."

"Not necessarily."

"Of course she did."

"Well, perhaps –"

"Don't tell me it didn't cross your mind."

"Okay, it did."

"Of course it did. You just said you thought she was pretty."

"Just because I feel a woman possesses beauty does not mean I think about sex with her."

The American returned a smirking glance at the Palestinian. "With the way many Muslims treat women?"

"Okay, I get it," said the Palestinian, "I said it crossed my mind, but she was not much younger than me."

"What is 'not much'?"

"Six years."

"And you know this how?"

"She told me."

"I see."

"This was not the point of my story. It was the lectern."

"The lectern...did anything go on *behind* the lectern?"

"Yes – no, not like that – before every class she would leave a piece of fruit or water for me on the lectern. But none of her classmates knew it was her. She was always the first one in, and her gifts would be accompanied by small poetic verses. She would always sign them with her name and phone number."

"You never called her?"

"No."

"Why?"

"I was already involved, my life was too involved. Besides, being American, I do not think she would comprehend my life and my duties."

"And your loyalty to ISIS?"

"Yes, I know. I owe you that one don't I?" The Palestinian breathed deeply and stared out across the desert. "Why did I join ISIS? Not an easy question but easier to answer after what we've already discussed. I first —"

"Before you get started, tell me…why does it seem ISIS is just a formal induction into the common arena of hate? It seems like a place for all of the bitter to go and unleash their bitterness. If you're mad at the world or think you've had a shitty life, you join ISIS or Al Qaeda. After all, ISIS *is* synonymous with the heretical Muslim jihad —"

"Interesting…" said the Palestinian. "As you must know, groups and others like this are formed to further an opinion or a doctrine – a voice. It is a way for people to be heard who would not otherwise be heard. And ISIS has captured the attention of the world –"

"And caused negative opinions of Muslims – of good, honest, peaceful Muslims," said the American. "ISIS, Al Qaeda and heretical Muslim terrorists desecrate the Muslim faith –"

"You said that yesterday...and again I hear your temper rising in your words. Sometimes man does things he does not want to do, but feels he must. You think it is fun to hate?"

"I think you *want* to because getting along with everyone would betray the bitterness you feel –"

"You think that is the basis of our decisions –"

"Sure as hell seems that way, not only by your laws, but by your actions –"

"Are you going to let me talk?"

"It pisses me off," said the American. "The Muslim movement you advocate wishes to kill anyone who is *not* Muslim. The people you follow are all false! Look at your supposed leaders. They are cowards who have conned all of you. How do you know that you are all not just tools being used by the globalists to destabilize the West, to further their ultimate New World agenda?"

"But when a people or a race of people are in a constant state of deprivation, with nowhere to turn, the one who steps forward offers hope, however little –"

"Of retribution? Of revenge? That's weak. We've already had those episodes in America. Jim Jones, The Branch Davidians at Waco, Manson....you're telling me you are easily manipulated – that they are manipulating all of you. That you are all a vulnerable herd of lambs. The same way you manipulate the Koran, twisting its words and meanings to justify what you do, like believing all those virgins will be waiting for you when you die – you've got to be kidding me! You think your Allah or my God will let you use women as instruments of sex? In Heaven! That's blasphemy! You slight your own God *and* women. You've got to have more strength somewhere than to buy into and believe that bullshit. Or is it that your people's nature is to go out and raise holy hell? And don't forget, after 9/11 much of Bin Laden's family were living in America – they even supported American politicians and universities. It is hypocritical to want to bring down the very nation that educated and houses your very own blood. All these groups now have enough money to build their own state and nation; build a great life for all Muslim people."

"Perhaps we are weak! Perhaps we are! Is that our fault? It is because of what we've known! I would love to have had what you had, but I didn't! I was without, and I got tired of being without. My family was oppressed. Yes, we are angry! Palestinians are throttled by the Jews. We want what is ours. And how do you know that your CIA didn't create Bin Laden and others like him? Or aid ISIS and supply them with guns? Maybe their strategy backfired, like in Benghazi."

"That would still make you a tool to further an agenda, which means you might actually be fighting for some of the same people I am."

For a few strides, I imagined the two men were silent over the prospect of that possibility.

"So you joined ISIS because you felt weak?" said the American.

"That is not the main reason I joined –"

"No it's not, and you still haven't given me one, but it's interesting how you change the subject and blame the Jews. It's always Israel, isn't it? Always comes back to the Jewish race and Israel with you people...you and your people are just never happy with what you have and you don't know how to live peacefully. It is all your misperception. The Jews *have* relented. World governments have relented. You have been given land. It has been recognized that your people *should* have a state. You were even given Gaza and what did you do with it? The government of Israel threw their own people out of their homes and into the street – they were homeless – and what did you do with it? Did you view that land as an opportunity for liberation? No. You mocked them and then allowed terrorists to move in, not peacemakers. All you want to do is to erase Israel like they want to do in Iran. You are all jealous of Israel, a nation of people that work wonders with little. And now, what will you do with the West Bank –"

"Are you Jewish?"

"No –"

"And yet you protect them. It is evident you are pro-Jewish; pro-Israel –"

"No...I'm pro-fairness – but even if I *am* pro-Jewish, why shouldn't I be? But you don't want to hear about fairness. You want to carry out obliteration! Don't you hear yourself? Your attitude? Your tone? It is your perception that Israel is the problem because you've been brainwashed and manipulated to believe so –"

"No different than your perceptions that the Muslim faith is evil –"

"No, not all Muslims. The heretics who murder and kill innocent people just because they are Christian or if they belong to a different sect – the way ISIS and Al Qaeda misinterpret the Muslim faith, *is* evil."

"You don't understand –"

"You're right. I don't understand how anyone can kill and hate the way you do. And the way you do it! You hit when no one's looking. You're all a bunch of sneaking, heartless bastards. Not one true man amongst you who has the balls to stand toe to toe with an American soldier without having his hands and feet bound." The American looked across at the Palestinian, and saw the effects of his words. "Look...I'm not you, but I *do* know right from wrong. There's always more to the story, I know. You just refuse to change your understanding because it's all you've known. Let me ask you this...are not most terrorists Muslims? Aren't you? Answer me. Aren't most terrorists Muslims?"

"Those people who are labeled terrorists, but we don't see it –"

"Like yourself...," said the American.

"Okay...yes...they are Muslim. But they have been branded that way by media and governments. Couldn't a bank robber be called a terrorist too? And serial killers? Couldn't you call Ted Bundy a terrorist? Or your gangs on the streets of Chicago?"

"Good point."

The Palestinian looked at the American with mild surprise from his response.

"But," said the American, "you said yesterday that we are both 'cloaked in the same material called skin' and we are 'under the same sky'...the people of Israel are also cloaked in the same material called skin...and they are also under the same sky as you and me, and in the end...death and the earth will not discriminate. Allah and God, who I think are one in the same, will not discriminate, and you, me, the Jews and everyone else on this planet will all be buried in the same soil. My dirt is no better than yours, and yours is no different than the dirt in Israel or anywhere else."

"We do not believe we terrorize. We fight for a cause just as you fight for a cause, only you do not understand our version. It is relative."

"*Your version* is targeting innocent civilians and stoning Muslim women who do not agree with you, and…you don't have any boundaries! No rules of engagement. You don't appreciate peace and love in a democratic society. You throw homosexuals off roofs of buildings. You loathe peace and love. Hell, Iran even banned Valentine's Day – a day of love!"

"Because we haven't had it –"

"But you say you wish you had what I had – what I knew growing up on tree-lined streets – why don't you copy our way of peace? You've had every chance to have it. All you want to do is hate and fight! Because it's the easier thing to do. You *have* to fight about something. Peace takes effort, but you don't want to expend that effort because all you *want* to do is hate the Jews and everyone else who doesn't agree with you. For you, it's so much easier to go on *hating*!"

"My Koran instructs me to oppose those who desecrate the Muslim faith, and who vehemently oppose it –"

"That is how you have *interpreted* your Koran! And you think that's the right thing to do? What about your tolerance? There are Jews and many other religions and people who oppose and criticize Christianity, but Christians don't kill them for it! Not in this age. Who the hell do you think you are? It isn't about religion. And I'll ask you again: Would any good God really advocate violence and death, as you proclaim yours does? You and your Muslim faith are just one big contradiction –"

"We are of different beliefs. No one is perfect. No one is right. We can continue to go in circles. The Mideast problem is more complex than you or I will ever know, and I was born here. There is no *one* answer because the issues that have contributed to the problems go back centuries before us, and none of them have ever been solved, so they keep compounding and getting worse, with new reasons forming.

The conflicts are as old as the olive tree, and they have spawned many new branches, near as often as olive harvests. It is beyond us."

"I agree with you. Then why don't you just stop?"

"Why doesn't America stop? I keep telling you, it is what I know. I am not proud of having to do what I did, I would have rather pierced my eyes with swords, but I felt I had to do it because of how I felt. My final decision to join ISIS came when I shamed my family. We have some similarities –"

"I didn't shame my family."

"No, but you have shame to share," said the Palestinian.

"What the hell are you talking about?"

"Perhaps you'll tell me about your home."

"Fuck you."

"That is what I mean."

"Yeah? Well fuck you again!" said the flaring American. "Don't shove that shit in my face, you spiteful bastard. You joined ISIS because you were desperate – that's weak."

The pace of their walking had slowed under the oppressive heat, heaved down upon these parts in a singular and constant wave, this desert being the sun's loyal conductor. The two men still had not yet grasped that their arguments were tinged with stereotypes and a failure to consider the spiritual whole of the situation. The American was right, it wasn't about religion – it was about perception, a programmed perception in a globally programmed society that only inhibited people; that divided people and led to opposing groups, political deception, and division. It was a program that did not empower the people of the world, rather it enslaved them – and most didn't even know it.

The heat, no doubt, contributed to their sparring and irritation, just as the uncertainty of their circumstance and direction contributed to their pensive moods, but yet they continued to courageously counter all expectation. Reading their story at this point reminded me of my younger brother, and my initial misunderstanding of his condition. He was born with Asperger's Syndrome. He was someone who also constantly countered and defied expectations. His quirks and idiosyncrasies soon became tolerable and endearing to me, outweighed by his countless other assets and personal qualities. Every day was a day in the desert for him, and I recall with clarity all of the hours I tried to help him walk through them, giving advice to limitations and softly directing a persona that was purer and more earnest than I could ever be. There was some success, but I adopted the failures as mine. These two men brought all of that back for me.

The American and the Palestinian continued to volley over ISIS and the Palestinian's membership. However, if it was possible to remove their respective nationalities and identities, then here would be two men – just any two men – walking side by side in the desert, with less reason to quarrel. If someone would have taken Asperger's away from my brother or cured him of it, he would have been just another man in the world. Just my brother, but *not* the brother I knew. Not the brother I loved. Not the brother I picked up when he fell down. Not the brother who pierced himself with the fishing hook or the clothes hanger, or the brother who I comforted after every temper tantrum, some of which resulted in streams of blood streaming from his head, some of those ending in our laughing together, with blood on both our faces, laughing at the holes in the ply board walls. Our love was our bridge. Our common space. For this Palestinian and this American, the desert was theirs.

"You were not inside my head during my decisions," said the Palestinian.

"Thank God," said the American.

The American sipped water from his canteen before passing it to the Palestinian. Meanwhile, a wall of fast-turning clouds was seen building afar, a force that extended from sky to ground. Both men knew what it meant.

They walked on, scanning the terrain for adequate shelter from what was coming.

"The problems of yesterday will not ever be solved! Because the people who created them are long dead," said the Palestinian, "but contrary to what you might think, there *are* Palestinians who want peace."

"I know. I am not *that* ignorant. And there are Muslims too…" said the American. "I'm also aware that there are some Palestinians who are Christian."

"Yes. Thank you."

"For what?" said the American. "So you're a closet ISIS Muslim from Palestine who wants peace, huh?"

"I have dreamt of it, but don't ruin my reputation," he said with a smile.

The Palestinian wrote:

> *The American's awareness was impressive. That we were able to talk in an unguarded manner; that we were able to trade half-smiles, was almost awkward for me, as if I was violating some pledge. Whether he felt the same I did not know – when he reads what I have written, I am sure he will think about it. His willing-*

*ness to give was something I was not used to,
even amongst some of my own, who hoard
what they have unless it is an open feast.
However, what the American does not know
are the many days that have been mine. If he
had lived the same days, in the same shoes as
my own, and in the same lands that I call my
home, would he have joined ISIS too? Would
he be a Muslim? Would we have been friends?
But I am starting to see that our humanity –
the energy that makes up our very souls – is so
much more than what we are arguing about,
making all of our respective causes so trivial.*

The men came upon a fossil rock with natural ledges grown out from its layers. It would
be large enough to shelter them from the on-
coming storm. The American took a poncho
out of his backpack and with it created a
makeshift tent, angling it close to a small shrub
that grew out from the rock.

After the long stand-off the day before, the
sleepless, non-stop night and having continued
to trek all morning, the men welcomed having

to burrow under the ledge of the rock. It was rather revelatory at first, coordinating a shelter in concerted effort, and working together in co-operative rhythms. It made them both uneasy. It was almost logically wrong. It was only the day before when the American and Palestinian were ready to kill each other. Twenty-four hours later the same two men were huddling under the same tent, sharing space, breathing the same air, and bracing for the fierce sand-storm that was bearing down on them.

The *Haboob* or "phenomena", as it is called, from the Arabic word *habb*, meaning "wind", is a monsoon-like storm with ancient beginnings in these territories, and as it bore down on the men, a look out across the desert, behind the rock, was enough to make the blood quicken – a complete and utter wall of dust and sand with wicked downdrafts that instantly altered the desert landscape. This one was a monster. The Palestinian described the scene:

> *It looked like it reached as high as the heavens and then fell to the earth, as if sent by divine*

Providence to scrub the desert clean from yes-
terday's death, memories of which still
lingered for both of us, I know. The winds
reached 60 or 70 miles per hour, blowing the
tent off us, leaving only our backpacks and the
rock shelf as protection. Our faces, already
scraped, cut and chapped, assumed a condition
even worse. Granules of sand and dust embed-
ded in our ears and in the corners and creases
of our eyes. We knew it would soon pass, but it
was no rest for our tired bodies, as we hoped it
would be; it was however a reprieve from our
differences, heaved upon us by nature, which
was in some ways ironic because nature was
playing the role of peacemaker.

The storm lasted about three hours and it
was a battle from the first moment to the last.
After it was over, as if snowed in from a bliz-
zard, the American and the Palestinian had to
dig out from a sand dune that had formed
around them, digging through desert debris
and arbitrary insects that were surreptitiously
transported there. It was not until late after-

noon when they had dug themselves out. The sun was still hot. Their bodies were still tired and now covered with sand and dust, blending with yesterday's mixture, and their limbs were aching, but they decided to walk a while more in the daylight.

"How much longer?" asked the American.

"I do not know. I'm starting to feel like we just *might be* the only two alive," said the Palestinian.

"Yeah, it sure feels like it."

"Are we any different than stray sheep...? Bewildered by the lack of any other human presence?"

"I don't understand it," said the American. "At least not yet."

The un-worldliness around them persisted, and it sent the American's mind wandering. He thought of summers in Long Island; that elongated part of New York that stretches out across the Atlantic. He felt the sensation of reclining on the lush green lawn, listening to the ballgame on the radio that was his "summer

106 · Neal Bogosian

radio", amidst subtle honey bee buzzes around the hydrangea bushes – the delicate, ever-working, determined creatures, darting in and out, drones working in the service of the female Queen, abiding by the orders of their destined and short lives. There were soft breezes and the smells of a summer cookout and all the rest of the scents he associated with the memories of summer. They were his past moments kept in safe storage; times that were harmonious and happy. He could hear her voice calling out to him, asking if he would like some just-made iced coffee or a deli sandwich or some ice cream or fresh lemonade...or kisses. *I'd love one of those.* He could see her coming out, and this part he replayed over in his mind, re-tasting, re-hashing the pulp of his own days. He saw her body, the body he loved and loved to make love to. He took in her smile, the one that melted him to tenderness every time. Her eyes, the ones to which he closed his own eyes on so many nights, hold-ing her smooth hand under the covers, caressing her skin, creamy and supple, every bit of her delectable in love. Her taste, her smell, her touch – he felt her lips on his…warm peck after warm peck, love after love, then, like a nocturnal dream that abruptly closes without warning, the American thought of *him*. *Him!* And it all went away. Turned off with the summer radio. The sight of his face washed it away, swishing and splashing into the Atlantic, where the south shore tide sent it turning and turning until it dissipated, its bitter remnants settling on the ocean floor…next to the rusty wedding bells and that *other* jaded day.

"Hey! Hey!" called the Palestinian to the American. "Why are you walking so fast?"

"I'm not…I'm just...I'm walking."

Even as the daylight hours waned, the heat continued to bear down on the men. If they could not kill each other, then it was soon evident that the elements would challenge them and try.

"I was calling after you. Are you okay? Your mind is full."

"What are you a mind reader? Teacher, philosopher, mind reader...*and* terrorist! What a fucking mix!"

The American kept his pace, forcing the Palestinian to walk faster.

"Why don't you just let it out! Say it! We're all alone in this great big desert. Get it off your chest –"

"Look!" screamed the American, halting his advance, "I will talk when I am goddamn good and ready! Do you understand that? You fucking act like we've known each other for years – you crazy Arab! You have no idea what is running through my head just as you said to me back there, about me knowing what goes through yours."

The Palestinian looked at the American, looked into his eyes, and said in a quiet voice, "It is eating you up inside, and I see it. That is all."

The American was uncertain how to respond to the Palestinian's words. He could only return a gaze, but it was enough.

The Palestinian wrote:

I came to know when the American was in pain; when his plights at home were stirring in him. He held them in the depths of his eyes, and whatever it was, was a punishing scar deeper than I could fathom, and if he were my brother, it still would have been deeper than I could reach.

His brother...and again I thought of my gifted brother with Asperger's. There were so many hours when I tried to reach him – I mean *really* reach him. His disability prohibited it, and I was only granted flashes of breakthrough. But he always finished with, "I love you, brother." Up to that point, he would perseverate on the holes he made in the wall with his head, or my ripped clothes, but as soon as he said, "I love you brother," it all changed; reality shifted, and the episode was over.

4

The two men walked on, into the desert.

"Do you think the peace that we feel here is everywhere?" asked the Palestinian.

"I don't think so, even though it feels like we're the last two men on earth. And I don't think you believe it either. Something's going on somewhere. I feel like I'm in the middle of a vacuum. Everything around us is so surreal. It's as if what we see is not what really is."

"Maybe we are – in a vacuum. Maybe none of this is real."

"Maybe we're already dead. Maybe *we're* the only ones who died...," said the American. "Even the colors in the sky seem too rich."

They continued to walk across the scorching sand. The heat came through the soles of their boots, penetrated the cotton headdress on the head of the Palestinian and the cotton bandana made from a t-shirt, on the head of the American.

It came as a relief that the sun was starting to set, but the day had taken its toll on both men. Temperatures in excess of 100 degrees rose off the desert in shimmers, as if the heat from the center of the earth was rising up to meet the sun's rays in a tribal ritual overseen by the gods of the sun, with Helios, Apollo, the great Aten and the Syrian sun god, Elah-Gabal, in orderly attendance; the heat, escalating in thousands upon thousands of streams, to join in consummation with the sky. The two soldiers walked into it, constantly through it, becoming part of it, one with the enigmatic prism of the desert, like watching grainy film footage of old bits of history, only these men *were* the history, and they still had no idea that it was unfolding in them, and before them, capturing them and framing them, in the ripest moments of time. On many levels, it was divine.

"Look!" said the Palestinian, pointing out across the desert.

"Yeah, I see it. It makes me feel better that you see it too," said the American, looking out into the distance.

The men soon came upon what had fallen into their sights: a small circle of one-room adobe dwellings, the evident residences of a nomadic group of people. The dwellings were partly submerged in sand drifts that crawled up the walls and sifted over the roofs, giving both men the sense that it was an abandoned community.

The American drew his gun. The Palestinian held his rifle at the ready. Both men then slowly advanced into the circle of single-entry homes – working in unison, as one unit. There were eight structures in all. Lurking shadows combined with fatigue and weariness resulted in anxious moments, the men having to endure and reconcile with what their eyes were seeing in the form of dark shadows and sand drifts; the forms were not hostile enemies, but signs of desertion. Before long, they had looked in each one until the area was secure.

"No one's here," said the American.

The wind whistled through the circle, stirring up dust and sand that swirled around the feet of the men, and it rustled up the traces of the occupants who once resided there, their fated moments and movements etched in a time that could only be surmised, but it was one that was recent.

They found a clay pitcher inside one of the homes that was still half-filled with water. The American took a purification tablet out of his bag and dropped it into the pitcher. The two men passed it back and forth until it was gone. Inside another dwelling, etched into the rear wall, was a primitive-looking illustration of a god reaching down out of a cloud, his arm outstretched, about to grasp the earth below, fire shooting outward from each of his fingers. The brow line of the god indicated anger; his eyes determined and his decisive action swift. In his other hand, above the clouds, he held another world, strikingly similar to the earth below, but whose colors were fresher and bolder, indicating a world anew, with a new sun in its wake. Arabic words were written next to the etching.

"It reads: *Man has reached all he can. The next world awaits. The next world comes, unbound and uncorrupt*," said the Palestinian.

The men could only look at each other in silence. The American wrote:

> *We were unsure whether to take the etching literally. Did it tell us about what was happening somewhere else? Was it the reason the dwellings were empty? Had they fled to prepare for some great coming? I know we both rolled it over and over in our minds. We weren't sure if, in some way, the etching was a prediction of our own future, regardless of whether it was a parable or a direct warning. Perhaps it was a clue to why we were alone. I thought of my parents. Then I thought of her. I wondered what she might be doing.*

The men hovered around the small dwellings for only a short while longer, trying to make sense of them. There were no other clues of the former inhabitants, perhaps whisked away with the desert sands and winds. The construction was old, but not ancient, and the interiors smelled more like beachfront bungalows during a hot, busy summer, than a small abandoned community in the middle of a desert.

"This could be a training camp," said the American. "They trained in the center here –"

"No. It is not."

The American looked at the Palestinian, but said nothing.

"Yes, I *have* been to one," said the Palestinian.

"I didn't say anything."

"Your look said enough."

"But it didn't say everything."

"Should we spend the night here?" asked the Palestinian.

"No. We can't risk it. The question I have is, *why have they gone, and where?*"

"I do not know, but why would they leave the water or not drink it after going through the pains of bringing it here?"

"Maybe they forgot it. It looks like a dune over there, about 200 yards out with some small brush," said the American, pointing out into the desert. "We'll set up there. Dig a trench."

"Tell me, my fellow American traveler, are we to sleep head to head...or gun to gun?" said the Palestinian, as the two men walked to the place that would be their bedroom for the night, under the starstruck desert sky that seemed to go on forever...and ever.

When I visited the area, long after the time these two men walked through it; when the world they once knew had indeed changed and boundaries had reshaped, I tried to imagine what it was like for them. I did see the night sky that they must have seen. It was majestic in every sense, as if the characters of the

Arabian Nights, with ornate and jewel-covered diadems, could emerge from the stars at any instant. The sky sparkled like a king's crown, helped no doubt by the uninterrupted landscape beneath, and the big, oval moon that hovered like the desert foreman, dripping on the sand and forming shadows in its slopes and weaves. The Adobe dwellings they wrote of were still standing. I saw the artwork of the god that they saw and remembered my brother's gifted ability in art, and how he exacted revenge on all of his most hated teachers, by drawing them in unflattering poses and settings. My brother would have marveled and stared if he saw the god in the dwelling artwork. He would have admired the detail and tried to incorporate it into his own work, only to come running through the house after he was done to show me, with the biggest, most magnanimous and proud smile. *I love you, brother*.

The Syrian Desert possessed some sort of mystical aura that impressed my mind and every memory in it, perhaps attained from the energy of the countless moments of history that it beheld, and now still beholds. This Palestinian and this American were now part of that history. When I stood on that desert sand – some parts rough and some parts smooth – if I imagined hard enough, I could hear echoes of their moments, their swishes through the sand; their unbridled conversation and banter that sustained their survival, at least to this point, and when I looked up into that night sky, if I forced my mind hard enough, I could see them in the stars, embedded there as part of the grand destiny of this great tempest, this earth.

After digging the trench and surrounding it with rocks and brush to trap their own heat, the men settled in. Under the top layers the sand was temperate. The American shared another MRE meal. *"Beef Stroganoff,"* he said to the Palestinian. "I hope you don't mind so much meat."

"Since I don't know what day it is, it doesn't really matter."

"So…you were in a terrorist training camp?"

"I was."

"Did you know those who were involved in 9/11? Or the Spanish, Bali, Paris, Brussels, or British bombings? There's been so many I'm sure I'm missing a lot in my abbreviated list."

"No."

"Would you tell me if you did?"

"Yes."

"Hmm…"

"What does that mean? You think I am lying again?"

"Here…" said the American, passing the meal to the Palestinian.

"Thank you again for sharing your food."

"You're welcome."

"Without arguing…what else are you now thinking of me?" asked the Palestinian.

"We're too damn close to argue. It would get cramped in here fast."

"So are we to sleep gun to gun or barricade ourselves with sand castles?" said the Palestinian.

"Is that your way of asking me if I trust you?"

"It *is* a trust question."

"Our differences alone would knock them down."

"Or maybe we might surprise ourselves and connect them – then we'd share an even bigger one…"

"Hmm…I don't think your fellow ISIS soldiers have that sense of humor…," said the American.

"What are you trying to say? You don't think we smile?"

The American sighed. "Yesterday my answer would have been, *only when there's death on your hands*."

"And today?" asked the Palestinian.

The American did not reply.

"Well, I guess I have proved you wrong."

"No you haven't," said the American.

The Palestinian was quiet.

"With the history of the Muslim faith, being what it is," continued the American, "how can you faithfully follow and abide by its principles?"

"Now *that* sounds like a question you've been holding in. And just what is its history? What do you know of the Muslim principles?"

"I know that even Thomas Jefferson wanted to wage war against Islam, against Morocco, Algeria and a couple others I can't remember, because the Muslims there were so barbaric. Muslim pirates used to abduct people and make slaves out of them, including Christians, or they'd kill all of the men and women who were non-Muslims and keep the young girls as concubines or sex slaves. They mutilated young boys and then made them obedient workers under their control. *That's* why Jefferson had a Koran; it wasn't out of tolerance, it was to better know his enemy —"

"Do not the Americans have their own history with slavery and shame?"

"Yes, that's true –"

"How you took the blacks out of Africa, bound them in chains and put them in fields –"

"The white man is not without fault and shame, but your history isn't only about enslaving those who are not Muslims. Don't change the subject. You and your followers are under order to give non-Muslims – like me – a choice, regardless of whether I am black *or* white: either convert, submit and be controlled by Muslims, or die. What kind of peace is that? If people aren't Muslims, you are ordered to virtually destroy them. To kill them. Is this your idea of peace? *UNICEF* reported that more than half of the girls in many Muslim territories and countries are married by the time they are 18. You have a twisted view of women –"

"You are just full of criticism aren't you? Some roommate you make. What about your Christian faith? Is it so perfect? Are you going to tell me that the hands of Christianity are clean? That it has always been peaceful?"

"No, it has not. But the Muslim history is far bloodier than Christianity's history."

"That is a matter of opinion. Don't forget the Crusades –"

"You take death and hatred to extremes. You celebrate death – you are trained to *love* death! Don't try to deny that. I've watched your people parade in the streets like animals – no civility. Little kids waving AK-47's in the air. No order. Raising knives and fists in the air. Are you going to dispute that?" said the American.

"No...I am not. We express ourselves differently than you. Is that a reason for intolerance?"

Reading their journal was like reading a novel – these two characters had many dimensions, many passionate contentions, and many troubles riding their minds; a slew of filthy differences that ran deep and were the very reasons for the global war that infested the planet. Each man took his turn at the podium or on his soap box, shouting an offense, a contention or a difference, some based in truth, some based in part-truth, some based on opinion or stereo-type, all of it adding to more derision, but still…they managed, and they emptied their issues.

"What intolerance? You're kidding me, right?" asked the American. "There you go with that bullshit again…and you're tolerant of America? Of Americans? Calling us the infidel? Is that tolerance?"

The Palestinian did not answer.

"Is it?" said the American.

"I cannot defend myself to you."

"Why? Because what I say is true."

"What you have said has been *mostly* true, but you cite isolated examples based on per-ception, a perception that has been influenced by news media, propaganda, agenda, and the ways of your government…some of what you say is conjecture. It is not fair. Your govern-ment does not always tell you the real reasons they go to war or occupy lands. Globalism and the Rothschild banking system has much to do with their actions, all in concert with the United Nations."

"I tend to agree with you about the Rothschilds – and all the other merchant bankers – but is it propaganda and conjecture when extremist Muslims in America want to spread the Muslim faith throughout my country until it becomes a Muslim nation? Is that isolation? My country is based on Christian principles, that's the way it is. If Muslims try to change that they are going to have the war of their lives on their hands, bloodier than any ever recorded, because believe me…you have not yet heard from the gun-toting evangelical Christians who are right now watching and waiting to see where the dust will settle. They *do* know the history of persecution and they *will* defend their faith at all costs – and so will I. They will not allow, without resistance, any Shariah law to rule their lands like Britain has unfortunately allowed. We aren't trying to tell the people in Iraq or Afghanistan that they can't be Muslims, or that we are going to put our Christian faith everywhere until it becomes a Christian nation –"

"No, you are not, but you are spreading your democracy and your ways here."

"And what's wrong with that?"

"Iraq was better with Saddam than it is now without. There was not a civil war in Iraq when he was in power. He kept groups like ISIS out. You Americans created the void for us to move in."

"You've got to be fucking kidding me with that one. He was a bastard. There wasn't a civil war when he was in power because people feared him and his sons. Saddam raped women, killed children, cut the tongues out of men and tortured and killed them," said the American, as pictures of massacred and muti-lated bodies appeared in his mind, limp and lifeless men, castrated and sliced, and dis-graced women huddled in corners, shivering in fear. "He wiped out entire families for gen-erations. His sons stole happiness from newlyweds, when they would rape the brides on her wedding day. They were beasts. All of them! And look at the way you Muslims treat women! Look –"

"You're yelling –" said the Palestinian.

"I don't give a damn! How can you say that? How can you not fucking see it? Are you blind? Muslim women are never treated as equals. In Saudi Arabia they're not even allowed to drive a car! In other Muslim territories they can't even show their hair! You stone them with your demented honor kills. You never walk *with* your women or wife – in your lands they are made to *follow* you. And who are the Muslim men that they are so great to be followed? Who are they? Why do you force women to cover their faces? You claim to praise and worship Allah – are you ashamed of his creation of women that you hide them as you do? That you cover their faces? How you live is cruel! Why don't you walk arm in arm with your wives? You confine your Muslim women and then you watch like jealous heathens whenever they are *accidentally* around another man."

"Our women are not seen as slaves as you so carefully imply! They are symbols of good will. They care for their husbands. It is their duty and it is not for you to comment on because you are not Muslim! You do not understand. We keep them pure and uncorrupted, unlike your American women!"

"If it's so great and dutiful to be a Muslim woman, why did your sister move to America?"

"You do not understand," said the Palestinian.

"That's all you can say. Do you *respect* their duty? Or are they tokens of fucking flesh?"

"You swear when you are angry."

"You're unfuckingbelievable! You're actually analyzing me –"

"Just an observation –"

"Fuck your observation. It bothers me what you believe in, and what you follow. In America women are allowed to be themselves. They are respected *and* honored–"

"But it was not *always* that way! In 1860's England, an Englishwoman who married did not exist as a legal person! Before 1920 American women could not vote –"

"That was almost a hundred years ago! That wrong has been fixed but you haven't –"

"And is your Catholic Church so perfect?"

"No, it's not – far from it, but I'm not Catholic. I am, on the other hand, a Christian, and right now, in Muslim countries, Christians are again being persecuted; killed, disgraced or enslaved, and I know that heretical Muslims would love to have that happen in America, a land of many religions. Buddhism, Christianity, Judaism, Agnosticism, Paganism, Mormon, Jehovah…even Wicca! Why is it that the Muslim faith presents so much more of a threat than every single one of those? Why is it threatening to every *non*-Muslim?"

"You said earlier that there are even Muslims who want peace. Why are you not talking about them now?"

"Because the Muslim extremists don't give a damn about them. It is the Muslim extremists who ignore them, who overpower them and kill them – they kill their own and you know it. Those who do not acknowledge their authority are seen as sinners or are equally disposable."

"Should I be impressed by your selective knowledge of Muslims?"

"I've done my homework –"

"Yes, and I suppose you will tell me that the materials you study from and learn these amazing insights are objective and not slanted –"

"No more slanted than your opinions of us, or how you interpret the Koran."

"You have much to say despite your country falling apart in every direction, from within, because of greed, selfishness and immorality," said the Palestinian.

"That's true," said the American.

The Palestinian looked at the American, impressed by his quick acknowledgement and admission. It was another small moment of revelation and discovery – when you learn something about someone, however small, that forces a reconsideration of previously perceived beliefs. "So, where has this all brought us? To what point?"

"Well…maybe that the human race is about a helluva lot more than just religion. Wanna play cards?" The American pulled a deck of cards from his backpack.

In the journal the Palestinian wrote:

> *There was what the American believed. There was what I believed. If it started to snow in this desert, would we both not think the snow was white? The earth round? A sweet memory warm and fond? I did not have an answer for him always, but it is not impossible, I fast learned, to see life from the same horizon with one called an "enemy"; to see and experience the same moments. Is he therefore really an enemy? Perhaps only due to a difference in*

perception, and if it is only an opposing perception and difference that causes war, how frivolous and foolhardy does that bring war to be, except to defend oneself or one nation? For whom — what select few — are we doing the ugly bidding? The question then becomes: What are we defending ourselves from or for? The security of a culture? A voice? A way of life? A religion? There are many similarities in our religions, despite the strife that is present between us. In Heaven, it might be said that we are of the same material. In the beginning as in the end, we truly are One. Why can mankind not see this and act from this in the interim, I do not know. I am now beginning to see that even I have been swept up in it — however this is the nature of being mortal, and this type of behavior is not uncommon. It does seem true that mistakes are the best teacher, for I have learned that extreme dissent has marred humanity forever, and yet, like the ego, it has no worth or merit.

"We are getting along are we not?" said the Palestinian, while playing blackjack in the trench.

"You're getting philosophical again. I can sense it!"

"I think you are just as philosophical as I am. You think and ponder life more often than you admit," said the Palestinian.

"What if you were amongst your men right now? Your brethren? What would you do? You'd have no choice but to allow them to take me hostage, and like the cowards they are they'd wear masked hoods when they be-headed me – while you watched. Then would we be getting along?"

"They might wish to play cards with us."

The Palestinian noted that the American called *them* cowards, not *him*; that he said *they* would behead him – not *him*.

"You must operate from a different part of the brain than I do," said the American.

"So what is the answer? Rather than talk about the problems, do you have a solution?" asked the Palestinian.

"Yeah...the heretical, extremist Muslims commit mass suicide and leave everyone else alone."

"And does America leave everyone else alone?"

"We are constantly asked to help other nations or to intervene in other nation's problems. Then we get criticized if we stay too long or give too little. My country is damned if they do and damned if they don't. But we never asked for 9/11."

"You are occupiers. You have military bases all over the world. You spread your western ways everywhere –"

"No. Bullshit. People copy our western ways everywhere, because it is the way of freedom. It is democracy. A country run by its people – well...it used to be anyway. Most politicians don't give a damn about empowering the people anymore, they only know how to take from them, control them, and tax them."

"*Control* is everywhere because your government is growing like never before. You have laws for everything that restrict your freedom. Even the showcase of your ten commandments can now be contested and removed. Your nation has become so costly that much is outsourced to other countries. Your middle class is eroding, resulting in a class struggle. Your rich are getting greedier and your children are spoiled. Political correctness is bringing your country to its knees. Houses are not as well-built as they once were because the wood is too expensive or the builder is too unimaginative and greedy. Your highways can no longer support your increasing population. Sunday joyrides are a thing of the past. Americans no longer think and ponder as they once did. They only live for convenience, no longer valuing their imagination and wisdom. If you post a photo of a rainbow on *Facebook*, it gets 50 'likes', but post something that reveals a new truth about living or that there are chemicals in the food they eat, and hardly anyone pays attention – maybe because they are too scared or too brainwashed. We know this. Believe me, I have done just as much homework on you, as you have on me."

To this the American smiled.

"Ah! Do I detect a smile of mutual respect?" said the Palestinian.

"I still think you hate seeing us prosper – you hate our liberty and you're spiteful."

"Stop saying *you* as in *I*."

"Why?"

"Because...," said the Palestinian, before tailing off.

"What? Are you disbanding?"

"Look, my American friend, I –" The Palestinian caught himself, he caught what he said in his unguarded moment, and the American caught him too, and in a whisper he finished, "I really don't hate you. *Hate* is an all too powerful word – a negative word. You do what you must, and so do I. You are who you are, and I am who I am. But perhaps the only reason we are here side by side is because of the actions of governments – not the people – and the greed of the few."

"But all's that means is we will continue to fight for someone else. And if I were you, I wouldn't be so fast to say you don't hate me. You hated me yesterday…"

"What is it that it says in your Christian Bible?" said the Palestinian. *"Take the speck out of your own eye before you take the speck out of mine."*

The American smiled in reflection. "I used to go to Sunday School. Do you know what that is?"

"Yes, I know what this is. You would assemble for Bible class after morning service."

"Yes. My teacher used an old, antique Bible for the class. When I graduated from high school he gave it to me as a gift. He used to go to all of my baseball games and root for me. He was very supportive. That verse you speak of is from the book of Matthew. I memorized it:

Thou hypocrite, first cast out the beam out of thine own eye; and then shalt thou see clearly to cast out the mote out of thy brother's eye. He made sure we understood the meaning of *hypocrite.* He taught the difference between conscious and unconscious hypocrisy. Conscious, *knowing* hypocrisy without reason was the worst kind. Yeah...I suppose we all live in glass houses, but we are always quick to throw stones...even when in love, and in relationships."

"Are you done taking the specks out of my eyes? The *beams* as you call them?" said the Palestinian.

The American wrote:

He brought me back to those old wooden pews. I could again smell the smell that I came to associate with safety and holiness. I could hear my teacher – Mr. Howard – telling me not to be a hypocrite: "Strive never to be a hypocrite. Hypocrites have a marred reputation for honesty. They speak out both sides of their mouth. It is never the measure of a true and honorable man! NEVER!" It was also my first lesson in the shedding of ignorance, a lifelong pursuit that I feel continuing even out here, where I realize how much of myself I still do not know, or perhaps I just never bothered to look so far within. I'm learning…if we stop and face ourselves, I think inner peace might come.

While in the evening trench, the American took an emergency ice pack from his bag, broke its seal and placed it on his tired muscles, head and face. It prompted the Palestinian to unfold the small mat he carried – on which he would pray – and sit, before he built a back-support in the sand and reclined against it, resting his shoulder and his own tired body. I presume it was by this time when both men were suffering from sun stroke, from walking in that relentless sun, as if it had hemorrhaged, causing its relentless heat to fill every pore of the earth.

"I watched Saddam's funeral on the internet –" said the American.

"I saw it too." said the Palestinian.

"Why were they all shouting and noisy, like a mob of lunatics? And then the casket opened and they were all quiet, they viewed him, and then they started up again. The noise!"

"It is a Muslim form of lamentation. They were also chanting. It is like a chanting prayer – a prayer to Allah. We all grieve in our own way. Does that make it wrong?"

"No...not at all."

"The Jewish people...they have their *Shivah*. That is their mourning."

"Yes, so what's the difference?" asked the American.

The Palestinian looked at him. He knew what the American was getting at. "Did you ever wonder," said the Palestinian, "how birds of many species can all share the same sky?"

The American smiled. "Is the sky over us bigger than the land that we live on?"

"Of course it is," said the Palestinian. "Have you noticed that families of crows will mourn one of their fallen?"

"I have. I accidentally killed one with a .22 when I was a teenager. While the blood dripped from it on the ground below, they squawked and flew over it. They squawked for hours I...I actually felt awful for days."

The men settled more into their sand beds, breathing easier, staring up into the waning skylight, and thirsting to know what lay ahead. However, each man still had burning questions to ask of the other, as if meeting someone from the other side of the world – or the other side of life, no one question always connected to any other, but rather a disjointed blend in an unconscious desire for acceptance and under-standing...and agreement.

"Let me ask you...are you proud of your government?" asked the Palestinian.

"That's a wide, almost impossible question, but I do have an answer for you. My govern-ment, like my country, has changed since 9/11. Right when those planes flew into the towers, to the true American, nothing else mattered. Everything that was going on in our lives suddenly seemed so insignificant. We abandoned all of our little private soap operas. It didn't matter who was mad at who, who was cheating on who...arguments we had the day before meant something entirely different the day after, because the only thing most people wanted to do was love...love and save everyone. But Americans have short memories, and those feelings didn't last very long. I don't know when you were in America –"

"I left *because* of 9/11."

The American paused, "Were you there with your sister?"

"We overlapped, but we lived apart. I had only been there for eight months. Then I returned back home."

"And your sister's younger than you..."

"Yes...but she kept all of her personal affairs from me – I didn't want to know any of it anyway."

Again the American paused, slowly nodding his head in thought. "That's...really strange." The American looked searchingly at the Palestinian before continuing, "Well…anyway…do you remember the song *Hero*, by Julio Iglesias? Radio stations played it constantly –"

"Yes. It was very popular."

"Yeah, I think it was the reason that song went to number one in the country, because all everyone wanted to do was love and save. Everybody wanted to be a hero. It was perfect timing, and the song was slow and sentimental, matching the emotion in America. We all knew that the country would never be the same again, that how we lived would drastically change. It was a funeral not only for those people that died, but for what America was. Like I told you yesterday…all of our rules and laws…a lot of them are now *because* of 9/11, and because we're all hyper-sensitive now, hyper-paranoid, and there are conspiracies everywhere. We're going 100 miles per hour and we're not stopping. It's like a societal illness. And *that's* one of the reasons our family structure is falling apart – that and technology. It's like everyone is short circuiting. In Amer-

144 · Neal Bogosian

ica, there is a sense of desperation in the air, and it has led to a level of selfishness that I don't believe has ever been seen before. We can all sense that things aren't quite right and they aren't the way they were, and there's more change to come.

"But these times are unique. I don't believe they have ever occurred, at any other juncture in the history of humanity. We have a collision of primitive warfare and technology – drones, robots, and soon there will be virtual reality. At the same time, we have a massive opiate epidemic that seems to be ignored, they let the FDA approve one Big Pharma drug after another. And now we have a tax on healthcare if we don't have it. It's disgusting. Am I proud of my government you ask…no, not anymore. I think God, Allah, Yahweh…all the gods of all faiths – they are watching, watching these silly governments try to cull the entire human race and implement the New World Order globalist agenda, erasing traditions and boundaries, and it might even include eugenics. But in the final hour…the gods will laugh and say, *we were going to bring the people together anyway, but governments are not part of the final plan; this is about the people!* Too many people have died because of actions by governments. We are missing the sanctity of human life everywhere…and I have a problem with that, because I was under the impression that I was here to help preserve it."

The Palestinian remained silent, but the monologue compelled the American to recall the ghostly picture he saw of the streets of lower Manhattan, taken by someone the day *after* 9/11.

In the journal, the American wrote:

The picture was taken on September 12th, and in it I could see the small mounds of ash and white, powdery dust on the sidewalks and curbs, that looked more like a snow storm that had just roared through. In the picture, there are two men talking. One is a police officer. The two men are alive, but hovering above them, and above those sidewalks, streets and curbs, are soulful orbs filling the space in the picture like the rush hour of death, invisible to the naked eye, but exposed through the lens and flash of a digital camera. They were there. The confused and lost souls of the dead; expired lives trying to grasp the reality that they were no longer amongst the living. I remember this photo. I remember it well, because I still wonder if one of those orbs belonged to my cousin. And I can still see, like it was yesterday, the parade of coffins. Oak-colored, mahogany, marble, maple, urns...they all parade in my mind now, next to green grass, under calm skies and decorated with flowers, and the sight of tears and shock, and the sounds of wailing and shock. For some lives, the flowers atop those caskets were the last flowers on earth.

After a brief cessation, the Palestinian said, "I used to think Arafat had big, wonderful ideas, but then they became just big ideas that got corrupted."

"Did you like him?"

"I met him once when I was a boy. It made me follow him, the way an American follows and worships a professional athlete. But then I got older, and my opinion of him changed. In the end, he was no good."

"No he wasn't. I heard he hoarded millions of dollars from his people – from you!"

"Perhaps, but life can be misleading and truth can be a lie, which is why it is not wise to quickly judge, and your president is no better…he underestimated us."

"You can be a real spiteful prick, you know that…?

"I find it difficult hearing an outsider criticize my leaders. It is okay for me to criticize my brother, but not someone else –"

"But it's okay for you to criticize my leaders?"

"Well," said the Palestinian with a smile, "that's very easy to do."

The American shook his head, a smirk creeping across his face. "I think the heat is starting to make you loopy. You know, right before that blast yesterday I wondered...I wondered, *what the hell are we doing?* If you think of a nation as a house, America is a house that is a mess right now, but the politicians aren't cleaning it up. I have no doubt that at this very moment there are terrorists in America plotting to attack it again, who snuck across the border, and they'd love to get their hands on one of those suitcase nukes from the Cold War...I'm right aren't I?"

"I understand your frustration –"

"But I'm right aren't I? What I said? You know more than you're letting on."

"I do not know more than you know. I am just a fighter, but you are likely correct."

"I think you might know more –"

"Then why wouldn't I tell you now? What on *earth* would I have to lose?"

"We should have nuked Afghanistan. The object of war is to win, not be politically correct and play public relations games – that's when soldiers die, like many now have."

"Hmm...you're calling *me* loopy. Do you think that is the answer? To wipe a country clean, as you say? Do you really?" said the Palestinian. "It is the policies of your government that have gotten innocent people killed –"

"My government's no angel, especially with all the Black Ops crap they're doing to the people, I'll admit. But we were hit, and terrorism has been alive and well since the 1970's and you know it. And it's Iran and Palestine that want to wipe Israel off the map. Do you think *that* is the answer?" The American paused. "No, I really don't think it is the answer. But I wanted to see what you'd say. I'm sick of war."

"We are now talking in circles," said the Palestinian. "There is so much more to this, and we both know it. I am certain the elitists of the world – like the Bilderberg's and Rothschild's – know the real reasons for all of this conflict, and it is nothing that the media outlets have told the people of the world. However, every moment is a chance to reverse course."

Their conversation had started to reach another heated exchange. Sensing this, neither man allowed their tempers or words to peak into a full argument, instead they both dialed their emotions back. In the journal, the Palestinian wrote:

> *Here we are, in close quarters, practically sharing a bedroom together. The American relented, and so did I. There was mutual restraint. "I don't want to talk about it anymore," said the American, and I told him I didn't either. He has great passion for his nation. He is a good soldier, and one in whom his nation ought to be proud. Nonetheless, we are both stubborn, and we both disagree. I believe it just might be our will to do so. If that blast hadn't occurred yesterday, I would have killed him, and he would have killed me...because that was what we were supposed to do – it was what we believed in. Tonight I am glad we didn't, that I might look forward to my sleep and dreams.*

"I'll tell you...," said the American, "I think there are some big shifts and changes coming down the pipeline of this earth, and it's not all good. It's something that I just sense. Time is short. Historians will one day comb over the years that we lived. They're going to study from about 1990 to 2030, and they're all going to scream, *Wow! Look at all that happened!* We have a collision of wills, ideologies, doctrines, and of course warfare, while poverty, greed and ego simultaneously persist; religious dissent and intolerance...science and the supernatural, and it may all be in the midst of some greater cosmic change, some great world renaissance from which we'll learn more about our minds and ourselves than ever before."

"That is interesting...*and* insightful...I think what you say is true. I already know that some men wish they were dogs rather than human because their suffering is so great, but I am also hopeful that after, there will be peace – even between us," said the Palestinian.

"Hey, wait –" said the American, "your sister...did she...," he was unsure he wanted to know. The Palestinian waited. "...did she by chance wear a gold scarab beetle for a pendant?"

The Palestinian measured the American's face. He tried to discern the anxious, almost fearful look in his eye, before he decided, "No." And he turned away from the American, looking off into the distance, in thoughtful silence.

Despite their exhaustion, the two men exchanged a lifetime of words that night, more so than any other night. Some might say it was because each man was too guarded to fall asleep right away, each having to be sure one would not suddenly outdo the other, but I believe it was out of genuine curiosity and the desire *to know* the other, and I'd like to think it was therapeutic for the men to talk about their issues, release antiquated preconceptions, realize common ground and expose their innermost troubles, because that's just what the American did – finally, he opened his scar, that part of his life that was the leech of his soul – the scar that made him look forward to deployments, but out in that desert was the perfect time and place to face himself.

"I loved her more than the world," said the American about his ex-wife in New York. "I'd have done anything for her – until I found out. When I met her, she was a smart, vivacious blonde beauty, but by the time I left her she was selfish and withdrawn…and cold – so cold she made me shiver. The very personality that once made her so pretty; so sweet and sexy, suddenly became ugly toward me, and I didn't know why – or what I had done. Maybe she was always that way and I just didn't see it – or maybe she hid it away so well that I *couldn't* see it. A part of me broke when she did what she did…I really didn't expect it. I learned that love and hate are very close neighbors."

It was clear by now that the men wanted to leave something about themselves in the journal, some lingering sentiments and background that gave their words a face, something for the imagination of the reader to chew and digest, not unlike the memories and keepsakes I've saved of my brother.

For the American, pushing the ballpoint pen across the journal pages must have been difficult. On this page of their journey, there is a change of writers. The American's hand is replaced by the Palestinian's, who writes the rest of the story...the story of how betrayal devastated the American and left a scar that reached his heart, piercing its chambers, and almost interrupting its impassioned flow:

> *The American had a friend he had known since grade school. He was someone the American deeply trusted and revered. At the end of his marriage, he did not lose one friend, but two. The American would learn that his wife had been having a sexual affair with his best friend for two of the three years they were married, including the wintry day he walked in on them. They did not know he was standing in the room. He watched in shock. Only when his newly ex-best friend got up to go to the bathroom, did they see him. The American knocked*

his friend out with one punch. He was not sure if he had killed him, but he didn't care. He told his wife to get out. She told him it was her house too. He said not anymore. She said he would have to prove this happened. He said he would – he filmed it with the camera on his cell phone. When his ex-best friend woke up, the American knocked him out again, before dragging him outside and leaving him on the front lawn. He remembered that when he walked back into the house, with blood on his knuckles, he looked up into the sky and saw a hawk circling overhead. He swore he made eye contact with the winged creature. It was like some scripted cheat. The smell of sex and perfume rolling in the air, of someone else's passion…in his bedroom. He remembered staring at the panties on the floor, slid off her legs or thrown off in the moment – that moment – the American recalled they were part lace, part satin. Those panties, the type or the very ones she always seemed to wear only on special occasions, on those nights she knew she would have sex or those nights and days when she knew she wanted to, all the other nights, when the sex urge didn't strike her, a dingy, worn or printed, unsexy pair did just fine. But while staring at those panties, it struck him...the fact that all their intimate moments were no longer just theirs. She was that way with someone else too and it made their moments one fallacious void that he was then forced to grapple with, and spin and twirl, in an effort to understand; to understand her, as he tried to register what he was seeing, the largest size of betrayal in proportion to the size of the investment of his heart. He felt separated from everything, even his own life.

But the encounter did not end there. He went back the next night. He waited until she fell asleep. He wanted her to know that it was no longer her game, but his. He also wanted – needed – to feel a sense of her touch, and one more reminder of their expired intimacy; to be in the same bed one more time on terms that were his – not hers.

She never heard him come in. She didn't feel him in the room until he lay down next to her. She woke up startled.

"Shh…," he said. "I had to," he whispered, "just this once more. Whatever I did to make you look elsewhere, to betray our marriage…to turn you away from me, I'm so sorry. I just needed to lie beside you one more time."

"It's…it's okay –"

"No…it's really not that I'm here like this, but I couldn't help –"

"It's okay," she said again.

"Do you remember when we bought this bed?"

"Yes," she said.

"I hid chocolate hearts under your pillow…"

"Yes."

"And when my grandfather held your hand the first time he met you…"

"Yes," she said, "I could never forget that. We went fishing. Do you remember? He immediately recognized your mother's bracelet on me."

"Yeah, and his funeral…he wanted to be buried with a picture of my grandmother, and brought to the cemetery in his 79' blue *Ford* pickup. He put all of that in his will. He loved you instantly, and that meant so much to me," he said. "I believed we'd be together till death. I'm so sorry if I ever took you or us for granted –"

"Shh," and she rested her hand on his. It was their first touch of intimacy in months. "I couldn't handle the pressure of *not* meeting your expectations…or of failing you. So I ran," she said. "You're so proud, and I'm a coward. I treated you the way I did, because it was a reflection of the hate I had for my own weakness – so I just wanted to hurt you, over and over again, because I knew what it would do to you. You did *nothing* wrong." She looked at him. "I'm not who you think I am. I can't meet those expectations. I know this because…you're just – you're too good for me."

Tears rolled down his cheeks. "I'll go now." He started to get up.

"No. Please, wait," she said.

He turned and faced her. His body hovering over hers.

"Just hold me," she said. "Once more…stay the night and hold me."

His arms moved around her shoulders. He lowered himself to her, and kissed her lips once more, a kiss that made his body shudder. And they moved with the night, his fate in the desert just months away.

"Just know that I've loved you every hour of every day of our marriage," he said.

"I know," she said, "I know."

The experience made the American wiser. He acquired a great amount of sentient wisdom, but it was not of the happy variety; it was more jaded than that. And so he was, as he sat with the Palestinian out in the desert, well-versed in life's disappointments, battle-worn and weary of its falsities that have seemed to riddle and possess countless lives before him. Fractured love is *not* a unique experience in the concourse of humanity, but this fact does not lessen the blow, for not a single soul who has walked this earth ever leaves it without some immeasurable degree of pain or suffering, albeit relative in nature.

"I feel like I have nothing left to give," said the American. "I'm emotionally spent and depleted when it comes to love. You learn a lot about a woman when you live with her, but you learn even more when you break up, especially about yourself. It kind of helped me to know what I was made of; my thresholds and tolerance, how much emotional pain I could withstand, and how it felt going through me. On many days it's felt like a slow suffocation over every part of me. I was anxiety-ridden for a while. I had to get used to moments of quiet that didn't used to be quiet. In the process I learned to live alone. I keep myself occupied with all of the interests I have: reading and research, carpentry, going to the gym...I just don't think I can handle another heartbreak, not anytime soon. Memories of her won't leave me though, especially out here. It's funny how the mind buffers all of the pain. It protects you from bottoming out in grief. So, what I recall are the good times...that first year of our marriage. I have fond memories of it and I've convinced myself that it was with someone else, someone who really did love me...instead of someone who was scheming behind my back. I learned there are different degrees of love, and that she never even had the capacity to reach mine – she basically admitted it. It's also the reason why I'm forever reminded of Sanaa – the woman I let walk away from me. I know *she* loved me."

Nightfall cascaded over them. A pitch black silence that only contributed to the surreal reality that engulfed the men, but it was ideal for slumber.

About sleep, the Palestinian wrote:

When I was a boy growing up, it was sometimes impossible to go to sleep with a light on.

> *In my land, this is a sign of extreme poverty –*
> *to sleep without light, but some nights, we did*
> *not have any oil – we could not afford it; the*
> *result of choice between food or light.*

I don't know how much sleep they got that night, but it could not have been much. Morning must have come fast with the next day's sun blaring and descending down upon them, greeting them with a pale, depleted awakening. It was a heat that was heavier than the day before. When they awoke, the men's garments were already damp with sweat and it was harder for them to get going again; to move their achy limbs and to resume their journey towards those inevitable moments that awaited them, not unlike the inevitable moments that await us all.

"Yesterday you mentioned the treatment of Muslim women and how we perceive them. Men *are* preferred in Muslim families," said the Palestinian. "I will tell you of a very ancient blessing that is often said when we say good-bye to male friends: *May the blessings of Allah be upon thee, May your shadow never grow less, May all of your children be boys and no girls.* Boys are exalted in my culture. It is the way it is and always been. In America, you also have a tendency to see women as objects of pleasure or playmates –"

"So *this* was eating at *you* all night, huh? This is the conversation you want to start the day? In context you are wrong. Women represent a level of beauty and grace that no man I know can ever be. Granted, a woman's actions and personality can make her less attractive, but the same is true for men. There's been a double-standard that I think is bullshit," said the American. "I personally think women are stronger than men, and I don't see them as objects – not at all. In America it is often a mutual arrangement – and from living there you ought to know that. They act on their own choice. *Choice!* If they want to get up and leave, they can, and if they are forced beyond their will, it is a crime. Muslim women dare not get up and leave because they know they will be shamed or killed or beaten. They remain in silence out of fear. It's how extreme Muslims keep their people faithful – out of fear. How do you know your Muslim women don't want to leave? What makes you think they want to be suppressed?"

"They accept their duty –"

"On whose terms? How do you know they *want* to accept it? How? If they speak out then their lives are finished!"

"I cannot answer you."

"I'm not surprised that you cannot. You are cruel to your women and it has gone on for centuries, and because of it, they may not know any better. Many young Muslim men act like uncivilized beasts –"

"Boys increase the size of the family," said the Palestinian, "they earn wages –"

"Because you have made it that way! Women in America earn wages too! They work! They provide! And half the time better than men can! Did your sister feel the same way you do? Did you control your sister like this?" The Palestinian was silent. "Would you watch her get stoned to death?" the American continued. "Let me know when love comes into the picture," said the American.

"But...," said the Palestinian, "we also want boys because according to our faith no one knows when the return of Muhammad will come. Any one baby boy could be *Him* – and we expect it soon; the 12th imam, the *Mahdi* –"

"And what? Muhammad doesn't like women? He doesn't have reverence for *all* sexes? Are you kidding? Even I have more re-spect for Muhammad than that, and it's not even my faith! And then I suppose you want to see the winged horse in the sky?"

"There are winged horses in the Christian faith as well."

"But aren't they only in *Revelation*?" said the American.

"Are you suggesting that if we both see our winged horses it will be the end of the world?"

"Maybe it will be. The world that *we* know anyway. I don't believe there will ever be an absolute end to this earth. You never answered me about your sister."

"I love my sister," said the Palestinian finally. "*No*, to all of your questions...I could *never* watch her get stoned to death."

The men walked on, and it was on the third day when the real battle commenced. The American wrote:

> *Every step today is an effort. I can feel my skin starting to burn and my body dehydrating, but we have to conserve the water, and I don't have much left. I'm thirsty and my head aches. After walking so much in the sun, I now smell like the sun and look like the sun — I feel like I have become, in these recent days, an adopted child of the sun.*

The heat affected the American more than the Palestinian, but both still felt it riddling their faculties.

"So..." started the American, "Why was it again that you joined ISIS?"

"I thought that I —"

"No, you didn't. You didn't tell me all of it. What made you leave home?"

The Palestinian looked at the American and smirked. "In the Koran, in *Surah II* – the prophet *Hud* – it reads: *If we give a man a taste of Mercy from Ourselves, and then withdraw it from him, behold! He is in despair and falls into blasphemy. But if We give him a taste of our favors after adversity has touched him, he is sure to say, "All evil has departed from me." Behold he falls into exultation and pride.* I did not marry the woman who my father wanted me to marry, and in a fit of anger, I hit him. It is a sin to be disobedient to one's father – it is punishable. When I hit him, I disgraced myself in my younger brother's eyes, who looked up to me, so I felt double shame. I considered everything for one long, sleepless night. With my eyes open and filled with tears, staring at the ceiling, and seeing only one color, I could think of only one alternative. Before sunrise I left home. About one month after I left, I learned through a friend that my brother had cancer…," said the Palestinian, his voice trailing off.

"And how is he now?" asked the American.

"I don't know," said the Palestinian, his eyes again filling with tears. "I was too afraid to find out."

"He could be fine –"

"He could be dead!" said the Palestinian, stopping in the sand and turning to face the American. "I have found it difficult to live with me. Can you understand this?"

"Yes…"

"I have shame, but I also have principles *and* beliefs."

The men resumed their walk in silence, except for two words: "I'm sorry," through the lips of the American.

As soon as I read the American's apology and expression of sympathy, I had this flash-back: I'm sitting at the dining room table.

There's my mother. My father. My brother. The solar skylight overhead giving us energy, warmth, and illuminating everyone's faces. My brother is wearing a collared shirt – he always wore collared shirts because he liked to turn up the collar. He motions to me to turn my collar up. Since he is non-verbal, he indicated this with a grunt. "Honey, you know your brother doesn't like to turn up his collar," said my mother. My father only looked on with a kind smile, worn and weary from working all day in the garden, and other reasons he never wished to speak of; I knew it would make my brother happy if I turned up my collar, and it would extinguish a possible episode. So I did it, and my brother smiled his great smile. There were two pieces of apple pie left in the dish, at the center of the table. I instinctually reached for one. That was it. I reached for the wrong one. My mother tried to stop me with an inconspicuous, incomprehensible vocal response that rivaled my brother's grunts. It was too late. I already touched the wrong piece. My father instantly stood up in my defense. Before I could say I was sorry, my brother started for me. My father intercepted him, and took him to the ground. By this time in life, we were all out of words; there were only a few that worked anymore. "I'm sorry. I love you, brother...I love you," as he kept swinging at my father who was in full defense mode. Then I remembered the woman he met at the market earlier that day. Her name was Kaia, and my brother couldn't take his eyes off of her. Whenever he got excited he would pull down on both of his ears, like they were handles or straps on a subway. Anyway, in that moment it was leverage – ammunition to get him to stop, "Remember Kaia? Remember?" My brother paused and looked at me. "If we are going to invite her over, you need to sit calmly at the table. She would not like to see you like this. And I don't want any apple pie. I'm very sorry that I touched yours. So now you have *two* pieces. I love you, brother." And I finished with a smile that matched his. It was enough. He started to pet my father's head; his signal that he was done. Not five minutes later, while my father tended to a bloody lip he got from a right hook, my brother sat calmly at the table, hands politely crossed, as though he was waiting to speak to a dignitary. He stayed there all night, until he fell asleep in the chair. Two pieces of apple pie remained on the table. He had placed each piece on a clean, white plate; one for my brother, and one for Kaia. Doctors said my brother's autism came from my father – it was in his genes. They even identified when it got there – around the beginning of the 21st century.

The desert elements continued to wear on the men. The American developed sun blisters on his neck, while the skin on his back felt like a slab of dry cement. Respectively, for both men, their sun stroke worsened. Their temples throbbed like hammers, and the ache in their heads mounted, but they continued to move. They moved and they kept moving…they went *in* movement, *to* movement, and they went deeper into the desert. All they could do was get closer to the other side, to the waiting, wanton mouth of life, and to the ways of the human race that would meet them when they got there. They continued to step, trekking and sloughing through the scorching desert sand, stepping and stepping, while the taxing weight of lifting each foot out of the sand, before pushing off again, quickly multiplied, to the point when their legs felt like columns of lead. The way one walks is a sort of signature of the individual – the Palestinian's gait; the American's gait – and somewhere therein, traces of their parental stamp, both men no doubt born into the world amidst a glint of glory to proud parents. However, their respective upbringings could not have been any more different, nonetheless, here they were still trekking side by side.

With the name of God or Allah constantly on the lips of most Arabs – most Muslims – this Muslim from Palestine also echoed the same regard, both consciously and unconsciously. It was his constant prayer, spilling from the mouth of his mind.

The Palestinian wrote:

> *My mind was full and getting fuller. I wondered and walked. I wondered more than I ever have. I sorted through my mind, wrestled with the torturous guilt that it held, and decided to surrender, for guilt is a thing that cannot be erased, but only eased; it is something to give into, and only then does it begin to mend – a mending from dissipation; a dissipation from surrender. I must forgive myself, as the American must also forgive himself. The vagaries of both of our fates were not just experiences, but lessons of the self. It is where wisdom is born, however painful it is to attain...and admit. In this way, we are common, and united. Our spirits are greater than any worldly issue, this I know for certain.*

174 · Neal Bogosian

The men came upon a deep, sunken depression in the desert sand. They weren't sure if it was a sinkhole, and they tried to trek along its outer edge. Lying in the center of the steep depression, was a camel carcass. Flesh was still on its bones, and a knapsack was still strapped to the camel's back.

"What the hell is going on?" said the American.

"I don't know," said the Palestinian.

The American tied a rope around his waist and gave the other end to the Palestinian, before venturing further into the hole, until he was within arm's length of the camel. He reached in, fighting flies and maggots, and untied the knapsack.

"Why? Why would they leave this here?" said the American, after he emerged from the center of the hole.

"The camel might have been sick or injured, or maybe it wandered away and got lost, because I do not understand why anyone would leave their goods behind. As you know, out here it is not a wise decision."

"The smell makes my headache worse."

The American wrote:

Seeing the camel made me anxious. It made me feel like I was losing perspective. The heat has begun to play with my mind, but it has not overtaken it. We are still puzzled by the absence of life out here. I cannot say what exactly the state of the rest of the region is. More than ever we want to know what awaits us. From time to time, we do see birds out here. They are the only life we do see, and even they seem to be scattering, in some great, panicked rush to get somewhere, some place far away from the desert, but we do hold them in our sights when they are seen, and I think we both read fear in them. We have yet to see them land. They are always airborne, always in flight, away from us. What do they sense that we do not, as they fly in an unbroken stream across the sky?

Also tied to the camel's back was a blanket and sleeping mat, along with small bags of nuts, raisins and grain, and a sesame candy bar, all of which were still useful and edible, but there was not any water. Several feet away from where the camel had fallen, was an empty canteen, which added further mystery to the scene because it confirmed the camel had not wandered off – the canteen was emptied and thrown…as if someone was in a hurry to get out of the desert; perhaps the camel was pushed to its limits, and died from exertion.

The men soon resumed their trek, eating lightly, slowly…chewing in a fashion as lazy and depleted and worn as the heat made them feel. It was around this time when the Palestinian reached into his satchel and took out a bottle of water…it was a bottle of *Poland Spring*, bottled in the U.S.A.

The American abruptly stopped walking at the sight. At first the Palestinian did not realize that the American was no longer beside him, and the clicking of the plastic safety cap could be heard – the twisting of the top and the opening of the bottle. Five or six steps ahead of the American, the Palestinian turned around, with nothing but oblivious innocence in his expression. He looked at the American, saw his eyes and then, slowly, looked back down at the label on the bottle.

"Where'd you get that...? Where?" said the American. "You son of a bitch! Where'd you get it! You have *plenty* of death on those hands, don't you? You filthy bastard...," he finished with the word *bastard* still stuck in his throat, colored with presumption.

The Palestinian said nothing.

Suddenly, all that filled the American's mind were the faces of his dead friends – the comrades he couldn't protect: Fitzgerald with his Hollywood profile and blue eyes; DeMatteis and his look of relief; Betters and his look of yearning as he fell to the ground; Kourmpates and his charred body; Nemachek amidst metal wreckage; Bonderman and the painful crease in his brow from the single bullet hole in his head, and a single, poignant trickle of blood streaming down his temple; Bloomberg with his eyes turned up; McClintock still smiling; Murray and his kind-looking cheeks; Ricci and his happy face; Hochman and Hinson with the graces of acceptance in their stoic eyes and stoic mouths. The American pondered, *Should I kill the bastard for them? Should I avenge all my fellow Americans right now and blow this terrorist bastard out of the sand? Then we'd win – I'd be the last one alive.*

Despite his ebbing strength and blistering skin and heat stroke and dehydration, with his eyes red and raging, he charged the Palestinian at full speed and drove him into the ground so hard the Palestinian lost his breath.

"You mother fucker!" screamed the American, as he pummeled the face of the Palestinian, blow after blow, the *SPAT* of knuckles to cheeks, jaw, head and eyes, skin and vessels breaking and blood flying, quickly staining the desert sand. "C'mon you son of a bitch! Fight back! Fight…back!"

The Palestinian tried to put up his arms in defense, tried to fend off the American, but his attempts were useless because he did not have the rage and fury of the American, he did not have the fresh injury of heart and of pride and of loyalty…he did not just suffer the injury of a fractured bond.

The American grabbed the Palestinian by his shirt and then by his injured shoulder, and the Palestinian let out a painful wail that surely echoed as far as the next desert dune. The American stared into the Palestinian's bloody face, "So is this the time when I waste you, you bastard? Huh? HUH!" He threw him back down to the ground. "You are trained to love death. Well, I'll show it to you." The American reached inside of his boot and pulled out a knife. The Palestinian's breathing was heavy, desperate…and his arms lay limp on the sand. He was helpless…helpless and bloody.

The American gripped the knife with the fervent acrimony that funneled through him, traveled through every vein and transformed him. In his grip was the residual, stored-up anger from hundreds and hundreds of unresolved pains; hours and hours and hours that spanned years, all the way back to his last true day of happiness, but in the midst of rage, something odd occurred to him. It struck him that he had not come as close to re-attaining that old peace as he did when he was walking through the desert, alone, with this Muslim from Palestine, and he hated this fact. Hated that it penetrated his psyche at this moment. He let out two insufferable screams that bellowed throughout the space. They were screams that were sprung free from the bowels of his own private hell. "Ahhh! Ahhh!" He screamed again as he raised the knife to a striking height above his ear. "Ahhh," he screamed again when he plunged the knife down, purging his anguish. There was a brief sound of penetration – of piercing separation – trespassing through, thrusting and engulfing all of life; a revisitation of pain, hoping to grasp harmony. The blade was sent, ordered with force...into the sand just beside the Palestinian's head. The American sat back on his tailbone, driven there by the forces of emotion. He arched his face to the sky, and cried. He wailed his painful wails, scattered his painful cries, splitting the silence around him. He sobbed like a shameless, faultless child who had run out of options and could think of nothing else to do, emotionally beside himself, realizing the magnitude of his immersion into an alien and unfamiliar situation, as a soldier of war, only he did not know what kind of war he was now in, if there still *was* one. What was he now the representative of, out here in the desert?

The American picked himself up and started walking unsteadily to nowhere, weaving in the milky desert abyss, sobbing, urged on by a collision of emotions that included surprise and confusion. Everything that was in his head and in his heart converged on him, compounded by the question that riddled him: *Why did he feel listlessness toward raising his weapon to his en-*

emy? It was as if he was violating some pre-programmed pact. It bothered him. His outburst confronted and opposed that which had been ingrained in him. He had suddenly become a contradiction to everything he knew and was taught, but it ignited the truth within him; it was his true self that emerged.

I believe it was at that moment when both men finally superseded war and religious strife, and entered the next world of humanity, harmony, and love; love as a frequency, for it is not relegated to romance, but also healing and vibration. Love has the power, at a cellular and molecular level, to permeate even the staunchest of souls.

The American turned toward the Palestinian, who was still lying motionless on the sand. "What the hell is going on? What are we doing here? Why are we here? Why did *we* survive? Where the hell is everyone else?" He arched back up toward the sky and screamed, "WHERE?" Looking up, he could almost see Sanaa's face in the clouds – the Palestinian woman of his regrets. It made him want to kiss the sky with longing, all smeared with blue. Just then, a lone desert lark flew over their heads. Urgency was evident in its flight across the desert.

The Palestinian turned his head weakly to face the American and he mumbled something inaudible.

The American walked back to him, and on his way there, he picked up the *Poland Spring* bottle, half of its water having spilled to the sand, and he brought it to the Palestinian.

The American helped the Palestinian to sit up, and then he helped the Palestinian to drink the water. Again, tears rolled down the American's face.

"Do not...do not cry," said the Palestinian. "I...I understand you. I forgot I had...I forgot..."

"Shh..." said the American, when he came back to clean up the wounds he had made. As he helped to clean the Palestinian's face under the hot, omnipotent sun, he caught his mind daydreaming about home, about rolling out of bed after sleeping in on a blustery Saturday morning, to the smell of warm maple syrup. Fall was his favorite season, and he could smell and taste the season and the moments all over again, melting down over him, the same way he could taste and feel her kisses on his lips, while the city streets stayed busy and the brisk air snuck in under the guise of a whistle, through the cracks in the old window panes. The morning kiss and the tender morning stroke of his cheek, an endless greeting to start a new day, from the woman that secured his soul and brought a sparkle to his eyes. He could see her in her morning robe that looked more like a flowing gown, and smell her perfumed scent that was the natural scent of her skin, but to him it was sweet and always fragrant; an exotic trip of the senses, and to him she smelled like she was his and only his, like something that he was meant to have, shared with no one, both owned by the other's love. He beamed in the immersion of his own ardor;

the rising, the peaking, the cataclysm…how he would move with her, their bodies in unison, and how it felt to have her envelop every ounce of his being, only to feel reborn over and over again, like the morning dawn. It all washed down over him. It all was true – *his truth* – at the time. And now, after countless hours in the desert, gripped by confusion and mild hysteria, the two central women in his adult life ran together in one memory. All of the happy times – only the happy times – blended and twisted into one long strand.

"What was your home life like? What was it like when you woke up in the morning?" asked the American of the Palestinian. "I…I want to know…I need..."

The Palestinian looked into the American's eyes before resting his hand on the American's arm, and between swollen lips he uttered, "I will tell you…"

The Palestinian told the American about his own mornings, peaceful risings interspersed with the horror of falling bombs or mobs rioting or people chanting or bulldozers crushing and plowing through settlements. He enjoyed licorice tea, especially with his secret girlfriend whom he shielded from his family. She was older than him, a childless and lonely widow who was still too young to be alone and too beautiful to get old. He loved taking afternoon naps with her; her head on his chest, wisps of her hair in his face. He would always sleep longer than she would, and he would awaken to the smells of three of his favorite dishes: *Musakhan*, *Shakshoukeh* and *Hwerneh*. "Our loving was an easy love," said the Palestinian. "We made love in calmness. She had been through much and we both never took for granted what we had – our bond. Our touching of bodies and souls. We loved truly, in a way that was even greater than passion. We filled each other's voids, filled the craters in our hearts and organs that were put there by pain and loss, and because of where we lived and *how* we lived…in suppression and hiding. We were like two old souls and when we were together it was like we were far away from this earth. The day of the physical altercation with my father, after I had struck him and left home, I went to her. I told her what had happened and what I was going to do. She pleaded with me not to, that it was me who kept her living… and when she told me this, I cried. She cried. She already knew the offense I had committed and the shame that I felt was not erasable, and it instantly sent all of our most precious moments into the past, far, far beyond our reach. I felt them slipping away, as if the memories had miraculously become physical objects. Sleeping next to her would not have the same beauty as it once did. Telling her of my shame and offense marred all that. And so I left, my sadness doubled…we kissed and I left…I looked back only once. She was there, watching as far as she could with damp eyes. How I hated seeing her weep. I did not have the strength to look back again. A few weeks later, just before I joined ISIS, I had a pain in my heart. I suddenly was not sure if I should join. I made up my mind that if she was willing to be with me...if she would marry me and agree to flee our land, go to some place where there was not war – if she would agree to all this, I would go get her and not join ISIS. I tried to call her, but her sister kept answering her phone, and so I kept hanging up without saying anything. Finally, after a few days of this, I summoned the courage to call again and talk to the sister. When I did, I learned why she was not answering her phone. She could not live anymore. I was the final break in her heart. She went to Hezbollah, got a bomb strapped to her...and went to Israel...she was to go into a crowded café. Instead, she – she walked into the street, away from people, but where everyone could see, and she blew herself up. It was on the news, her sister told me. They reported that the bomb *accidentally* went off too soon, sparing dozens of lives. But we both knew it was no accident. She did not intend to bring any other lives with her. However, when I heard that, my life went too, for we were woven in the same love."

A spell of silence fell between the American and Palestinian. The American looked out across the desert, trying to keep his mind straight, while trying to register and connect the story he had just heard with everything else. There were similarities. Somewhere he knew there was room for the Palestinian's heartbreaking story within the story of his own life. There was common ground, common pain, and like a jigsaw puzzle, the anecdotal pieces blended together. He pondered the possibilities in the best way that he could interpret them, before asking with urgency, "What does all this mean?"

"What are you asking?"

"You told me a story…about you. It was just as human as mine – as my story –"

"Why wouldn't it be?"

"But we come from different places. Different beliefs –"

"What did you expect?" said the Palestinian. "I am a human. Just because two men do not end up in the same place, with the same sentiments and values and morals – just because governments and boundaries tell us we are not on the same side, it does not mean we are any less human or apart, our frustrations are simply of a different origin. We both seek identity, and a place in the world among those we love. We both had the same childhood innocence that once held us and the shock and tears when our parents first spanked us, and the first bruise when we fell off our bike; the joys of receiving a first gift, the sorrow of a first loss and the thrill of a first kiss. We both felt them. We are of the same capacity...it is why I now believe – especially after being out here with you – when we kill another, we are also killing a part of ourselves, despite the fact, in war, we must kill...or else war, wouldn't be *war*. Don't you see that your church friend who preached to you about hypocrisy, about contradiction, never gave you the antidote for living in a world that's filled with it, but he was wise to warn you of it. It did give you less ignorance, and opened your mind...perhaps enough to live with me, here...now."

"Why me and you though? Why...why are you and me out here...alone?" said the American.

"Maybe we asked for it...maybe we asked for it to be that way. Maybe our deepest thoughts wanted to understand the enemy. Maybe we knew that we weren't really enemies, it was only because people tell us we are. Maybe the universe knew that you and I were different than the rest. Maybe this is our karma...and we were brothers in another life."

"Did you? Did you think you were different than the rest?"

"I never wanted to hate...," said the Palestinian.

"Are we the exception? Is this...what we're doing, is it empathy in war between two soldiers?" said the American.

"Or is it the feel of the other's pain between two men who might have been friends away from war?" said the Palestinian. "As much as you or I might not like to admit that because it is not a comfortable idea."

The American did not answer. He did not have to. Later, after sewing an undisclosed amount of stitches into the Palestinian's face, he helped him to his feet, which was when, for the first time, he paused and stared into the Palestinian's eyes. I think that when he did, he saw a reflection of his own relative humanity. Out in the desert, their division was indeed relative through their perceptions. It would be relativity that would soon define the new millennia because it helped people to better understand each other. Ego is the death of harmony...and the absence of empathy. And most arguments – and most wars – started because of ego that resulted in a hunger for power and control, or a desire to fulfill some prophecy that was certainly founded long before these men were born.

I do believe that had it not been for the soft, cushiony desert sand that absorbed much of the brunt from the blows, the Palestinian's head wounds would have been far worse and internal, and I'm glad they weren't. While reading their journal it was easy for me to be taken up in both men, and as they pressed through that stark desert, the closer they got to that inevitable time and that inevitable place, I found myself silently cheering...of course not knowing at the time, just when and where their inevitable place would finally be. Just for *what* I was cheering I was not yet sure, but I knew I would learn that about myself later, and so I kept cheering, not wanting this journal to ever end, for I felt that I was experiencing their days with them, just as I experienced precious days and nights with my brother, before he would also leave me. It was my brother who helped teach me the joys of living, and as I later came to understand, that was one of his purposes on earth. One of his life purposes *was me*. He taught me patience and he taught me love. His differences – his perseverations, fixations, odd habits and eccentric genius – set him apart from the mundane, autonomous traits that afflict so many; they made him a colorful, buoyant beacon in this world stadium. And *he* always thanked *me*. When I should have thanked him, he thanked me, for trying to revive our mother, one summer afternoon, while she lay on the kitchen floor, having been stricken with a heart attack. I tried frantically to do all I could, with tears streaming down my face, but not his. I tried and tried and breathed and pumped her chest, over and over, until my brother – my brother with Asperger's – put his hand gently on my shoulder, and said, "Don't you know? Don't you know there is no such thing as death? There is only love… and life." My brother…my dear friend, and the trophy of my life. In certain moments he somehow showed an almost ethereal maturity that was unlike any I had ever witnessed. It was as though a switch had been raised and a higher self instantly downloaded and took over. In those moments, he wasn't my autistic brother, but rather my spirited guide. His lucidity overshadowing his 'other' self in ways I could not immediately comprehend. But I did know that he was more complex and more amazing than anyone I ever knew. His spirit was already beyond this world – beyond this vast mortal schoolyard.

5

When the American and the Palestinian finally resumed their walk through the desert, their pace was slower, and their dispositions more serene, and more accepting. For the American, everything started to fall away from him, all of his burdens and problems at home, all of his prejudices – for what were they worth out in the desert? What were they worth now? What were they *ever* worth? He shed his worry, like trimming the fat off a life, reaching its core, its purity, experiencing the very embodiment of living...in its rawest form, and in that form, nestled at the core, was an indescribable solitude; an emptiness of mind. Only two things were immediately real to him – the desert and the Palestinian. Even his recollections now seemed too far removed to be real.

The American wrote:

I can remember my pains back home, but they are now distant. I suddenly realized that I was remembering them in habit – it was by my own doing. I was summoning my own pain without knowing it. Maybe because I never got over it, or got satisfaction, or a Band-Aid for my emotional wounds, but I did realize that I was the creator of my own pain. So... here in the desert, I let them go. Or at least I decided to really try. I decided to leave them here, bury them in the sand. And as for this man who I walk with...who I have walked miles with – I can say that my heart has surely begun to turn, to look the other way, and for the first time in a long time, I swear I can somehow feel it smiling, feeling relief and letting out a sigh; I can feel it getting lighter. I know I'll never agree with his ideologies, but in my exhausted, weather-beaten state, I am sorry for what I did to him, because I have felt it, and maybe it took me striking him to feel it...that warmth, of dare I say, friendship. I have learned that the weight of conflict is heavy – and also that I really don't know a damn thing. I've been a loyal soldier to some-one else's program, who doesn't give a damn about me or the common person, only their own agenda. They want us to fight because it helps justify their grand plan, and their riches. My eyes just opened.

After hours of more walking, the men were relieved to see the sun start to set into the horizon. They continued to walk, searching the desert and searching themselves. Both men knew that the time had come when their qualities would be tested, not in war or argument, but in utter survival. Their endurance, tenacity, persistence, muscular strength…and kinship, were being slowly exposed, baring themselves under the sun that had just as slowly become their nemesis; at once at war with each other, both men were now lured into a fight to outlast nature. There were no apparent ill-effects in their relations following the American's out-burst, but as the American indicated in the journal, only another dimension of mutual understanding and common ground. Another proverbial wall had fallen.

All of the words they had spoken, contesting one another, were thrust into the background. Where did this leave their earlier contentiousness, if anywhere? Could it be said that their amicability was a result of it? I believe the men had arrived at something more personal and spiritual – something more important within themselves, and between them. It was a conciliatory human bridge that was forged over turbulent rivers of hate, distrust and dissent, fueled and instigated by causes that were not their own. I believe their relations actually superseded human nature, and superseded what they knew of themselves, and it crashed the bar of impossibility, illuminating the realness; the raw, fast fact that peace *is* possible between perceptible enemies. Their arguments over the past few days simply no longer had a place between them. They no longer fit either man, like a shoe too small, or a perception of life too little. These two men had already come – or walked – far beyond it. They realized that in truth, there are no limits to this life.

Still side-by-side they continued through the desert. Their breathing had begun to labor, while their muscles grew tighter and more de-hydrated. The meaning of their own existence was fast descending upon them.

"I was just thinking about my sister," said the Palestinian.

"What about her?"

"She has terrible asthma. It always amazed me how she was able to take those cold winters in New York."

Once again, at the mention of his sister, the American paused.

The Palestinian looked at him. "Yes, I re-member what you said. *Your* Bayridge woman and *her* asthma."

"Yeah…yeah it probably was hard for her, she just never told you," said the American.

"Yes…probably."

"Running is...hard for them, especially in the cold."

"Yes, when she was younger she could not participate in the same activities –"

"*Sanaa...*"

"Yes, Sanaa...," said the Palestinian.

For the next few minutes, as they walked, the two men alternated between looking down at the sand, and looking up at each other, their minds spinning.

"I don't know about you, but this has been a mind-blow...being out here, going through what we've been through, and seeing what we've already seen. I feel like my mind is about to spill out of my ears."

"You wouldn't want to make a mess out here in the desert, would you? And leave me to clean it up?" said the Palestinian.

"Well, now just think...you'd be blessed with being in possession of my brains *with* yours."

"Oh, my! *Ya iilhi!*"

The American, with a smile on his face, reached across and put his arm around the Palestinian, like a man would to his friend.

In the journal, the Palestinian wrote:

> *When the American did that, I knew it was a gesture from his heart. I knew we had reached a new place...We are nearing a point when every movement is an effort. We are almost out of water and our food is barely enough for two more days. As for the heat, its effects are cumulative, each new hour compounds with the wear from the hours before. The American's blisters are worsening, spreading like some disease. Our muscles ache and our bodies beg for coolness. My lips feel like scales, but my mind still works and my heart still pumps.*

On this day, the men were forced to stop before they wanted to. The American's legs were suddenly ridden with cramps, and wincing and writhing in pain, he fell to the sand.

The Palestinian quickly went to the aid of the American, applying pressure to those spots in his legs that were knotted and tense with spasm. After the pain subsided, or rather, once it retreated to a manageable state, the men sought out a place to sleep for the night.

They barely had enough energy to dig a trench, but thoughts of a cooler ground beneath the hot top layer were an incentive to keep digging. Once settled, the American used what was left of a small tube of salve on his aching muscles.

The Palestinian wrote:

> *I am not long for my pen this evening, nor is my pen long for me. We are weak, and the American's cramps might have been our blessing to stop, for feelings of sleep have quickly spelled us both, although we realize it might be from our sunstroke. I pray to Allah for strength. I pray to Allah for strength for both of us – me and the American. En-sha-Allah! The time has come for faith in the powers that lie in unseen space to aid us...or death will quickly find us. Thank you, Allah...for this day and for the slight of wind that blows.*

When the desert heat dissipated and cool-ness came, the men with the desert slept as one, as part of a whole within creation, emit-ting cool, impersonal sighs through the soft night breezes. The desert night in which they slept was quiet and eerie, an eerie peace that danced on those faint desert breezes and brushed the sleeping cheeks of both men. The night was thick with blackness, throttled by ev-erything unseen and only imagined. The scent of the desert was the scent of the earth – a deli-cate, interchanging, alternating mixture of dry grass, tall weeds, sand, and the distant, never-dying smell of history. The desert smelled old. It was an appreciative scent, one that altered the taste buds; one that commanded respect and attention for its quiet power. As I re-read the journal over and over, studying its subtex-tual elements in preparation for this story, for me this night soon acquired a title: *The Night Before*, because that's what it was, it was the night before all else.

For this reason I wanted them to have slept well. I wanted them to have slept the best sleep of their lives. I wanted them to have dreamt the best dreams. I wanted them to have visited their most precious memories. I wanted to talk to them. I wanted to know them. I wanted... and I wondered if they had any premonitions of the event that awaited them.

The next day offered no relief from the sun, and there was no raiment thick enough for shelter. Its effects were felt before the men even awoke. Even before they took another step, setting back out on their journey, their bodies were already sapped and dried. It was only by spirit, coercion, and strength that they got their body parts moving and cooperating with the mental commands they were given.

Both of the men's instincts slowed. The sharpness of their faculties dulled, and their eyes stung from lack of moisture.

The American wrote:

Today it is as if our limbs need oil. We can already see that we'll need to fight to get through this day. We already know it will be the longest yet. I can't feel the back of neck. My skin is darker than a bronze statue, but it feels like raw steak and some of my sores are oozing. I have been slowly cooking...this desert like an oven.

I have forgotten the war — I just realized. The one that got me to this place, and I can no longer remember how long I've been out here. It may be the first time I realized, but when was it forgotten? Does this mean it has lost importance? I know...this has become a recurring question, just in different forms. I think it's just that my life — ours — has taken precedence...I think...and the peace I feel from writing this decision brings more. The peace I feel is a good feeling. Secure. Rock solid.

Long ago I accepted the fact that I could die. I live with it. It's become warm to me. But I have a different philosophy on life and death than most, a different system of belief...before I do die, I wish I could have just one more pizza, a good steak sandwich and hear the peace of the ocean while eating seafood at the beach; smell its salty breeze and lift my sun-beaten face to meet it...I can taste them now, the pizza sauce, the steak and cheese and sautéed onions...the lobster dipped in butter. I can hear the gulls overhead, hoping that I throw them my pizza crust or leftover bread, not unlike the roaming children of Iraq and Afghanistan who have begged for my food. Those waves crash over me, all of them. My mind turns over in this space, in peace. "Peace"...there it is again, a common theme in these current hours...my heart does throb... and if my mother was near, I'd hug her so tight...and oh! Of course...Sanaa...I just had to write her name. I may not get to do it again.

The Palestinian's face was swollen from the wounds of the day before and one of the gashes in his face opened and gave. With pain in his eyes, the American quickly cleaned and dressed it again.

"Thank you," said the Palestinian.

"After what I did…do not thank me –"

"You were defending –"

"It doesn't matter…we were past that," said the American, before turning to walk again. "It was done. I'm very sorry, and now the shame is mine for striking you – I hope I have taken yours away."

With effort, they walked on, weathered and weary…one sustaining the other.

"I dreamt of my brother last night," said the Palestinian, "from the other side."

"What did you dream of?"

"It was a vivid dream. It was real. His skin was pure and luminous. He was cloaked in light. His eyes were kind, forgiving…in my dream I told him I was sorry. He only shook his head and I understood that my apologies were not necessary. We were both in a seated position. Golden leaves were falling all around us. I could not tell where we were, perhaps some holy site, but it was beautiful. There were multi-colored auras, and love in its ecstasy seemed to be everywhere…," said the Palestinian, his words tailing off.

"What did you take the dream to mean? That you are too hard on yourself and your brother forgives you?" said the American.

The Palestinian was very serious. He looked at the American and said, "The dream was literal. It was real. My brother has died…and perhaps he died last night."

The American was silent and introspective.

"Before the dream ended, he gave me a warning," said the Palestinian.

"About what?"

"Something immense awaits us. He did not say what…or I could not quite make out his words."

"I don't understand…" said the American, "*us* as in me and you?"

"My American friend…whether it be the world, the region or us, we will no doubt know it, see it or feel it. I sensed that we are certainly in for an experience even greater than the one between us, and so we – me and you – ought to decide now, are we to stand side-by-side and defend one another? Or are we to separate and let be what may, should that time come?"

"Do you already know your decision?" said the American.

"Yes," said the Palestinian, "but if you need to think about it, I under –"

"I don't need to."

"Okay…so?"

"So?" said the American.

The men stopped and faced each other. They looked into each other's weather-beaten eyes. I believe that what they saw was enough to create an epiphany for both of them, a desert epiphany immersed in the depths of a bond unlike either man had ever known, and unlike most men *ever* know; a sort of bond that not only had the power to last one life, but all of those that follow. It was theirs, encased in a place beyond judgment. It was where they had come.

The American extended his hand. The Palestinian reached out and seized it.

"I would defend you," said the American. "I *will*."

"And I, you...," said the Palestinian.

"This could mean we go down together," said the American.

"I know...but we *have* been together, and I thank Allah, as I hope you thank your God... for this gift of realization, of life and release from old, expired beliefs...thank you."

"And thank *you*. You have helped me to see so much."

"Nothing that wasn't already there...for both of us. We just needed this desert, and each other to bring it out."

Their hands remained clasped in sincerity and earnest.

"What if...what if my God and your Allah really are one in the same?" said the American with a smile. "After all, we *are* under the same sky *and* cloaked in the same material...called skin!"

The Palestinian laughed. "What *if*?" he said, "What *if*? I think they very well could be. And I would not be disappointed."

"What if God – or that Supreme Being that is every God and every Allah – is *in* all of us? What if we are all gods through Him? It might mean that everyone has it all wrong, that there are no such things as religious enemies; that spiritually we are fighting the same side, and misinterpreting all of our holy books –"

"Stop! It might bring us right back, and you know it. We never did solve our differences, even though right now they mean much less. We merely understood them better, and why they exist, at whose benefit…and at whose expense. While we might be under the same sky, we cannot deny that we *are* of different cultures. And we are still products of this world of hate and greed and filth, that I hope one day is cleansed of all its dirt."

"True," said the American, "but maybe that is just His way of making it interesting. Maybe in the future people won't put limits on their faiths."

Just then, something in the sky caught the attention of both men. They looked up just in time to see a bright red meteor streak through the atmosphere overhead. It was immediately followed by a second larger one.

"What the hell...," said the American.

"I don't know what's happening, but we better get going. But I have to tell you something first." There was a brief pause before he continued, "my sister...Sanaa..."

The American waited, and I can imagine that his heart must have started to race. "What is it?" he said.

The Palestinian continued, "She *did* wear a gold scarab pendant around her neck. You need to know that...just maybe..."

Tears filled the American's eyes.

"Maybe...," the Palestinian tried to continue.

"Yeah, maybe," said the American. "And maybe that's how close you were to being my brother-in-law."

The next few hours were difficult – even for me to read. The men's strength continued to diminish, and for the first time, they found themselves truly struggling to keep moving. Between them, not much remained.

They stopped frequently to take small breaks, in an effort to pace their muscles and their breathing. The Palestinian wrote:

> *The most arduous of days. My legs are giving out. I stumbled, falling to the ground once. The American was there to pick me up. He put his arm through mine, and despite his own weakening state, hoisted me back up. We are famished, but would never be able to keep any-thing down anyway. The sun felt extra hot today, and when we looked skyward, we could both swear we saw two suns.*

Their walk through the sand of the desert was no longer a trek, but a trudge. The Palestinian stumbled...the American lifted him up.

Moments later, the American stumbled or tripped – the Palestinian was there to lift him up. Had either man been alone in that desert, I am not sure that he would have had the strength to carry on, but here, the men did it for each other, to finish what was started, and to finally uncover the unknown, or what was left of it; to ultimately give the laborers of hope, proof of hope itself.

I believe that somewhere in both men was the true and conscious realization of what was occurring regarding their collective moments on the world stage, and in the concourse of time – that their survival or the telling of their story just might result in the prospects of peace for tomorrow; a hopeful and altered future that would once again usher into the world that fervent blend of exuberance and zest for life, stirring mankind to once again be selflessly excited about the unborn days and years before them, and to perhaps regain the sanctity for living, for in the time of these two men, the perception of life had grown cheap, with death, terror, and slavery; sinister acts and self-ishness fueled by ego, as common as death itself. It was *not* a civilization to be proud of.

These two solitary men, trudging and trudging, limping toward their journey's climactic end, no longer opposing individuals or dueling enemies, but rather the representatives of a common plight – *the* plight of all plights; the answers to an investigation that had plagued humanity since its inception: *Can humankind find a way of getting along forever? Can humanity finally experience that grand renaissance of thought and beauty; that elusive epiphany through which emerges a healthier, more evolved version of conscience and perception of life, and in the process, its true meaning?*

One aspect of humanity that strips all assumptions bare and reveals the best of all truths, is this: Our universe and much of its people *are* inherently good. The people just needed to be free; free from 'the system'; free from the agendas, the controls, the chemicals, the burdens, and the preconceptions; free from the beliefs and ideas of others; free from the egomania, and awakened to their innate powers within. And this brightened, freer, and illuminated future began with these two men. This Palestinian and this American – through their journals; they were the two unlikely friends that started it all.

It happened in the afternoon of that final day. They were out of water and just about out of food, blistered, bruised and beaten, holding each other up, taking each step together, and each step now belonging to *both* men.

"Look!" said the Palestinian.

The American squinted his eyes and strained to see what the Palestinian was seeing. "Where is that?" said the American.

"I think it's Syria."

"Is that…what the hell's going on? Why is… we need to get closer."

The men tried to hurry their painful walk, lifting or carrying each other along the way, their knees knocking and bruising and their limbs occasionally giving out, as they moved closer and closer to the activity taking place over the Syrian border.

"Why is everyone...running?" said the Palestinian, when their sight was no longer impeded by distance and shimmering heat.

"They look like they're in a panic," said the American.

Off in the distance they could see people running. In fact, there was not a single person that they could see who was *not* running. But from *what* were they running? The answer came when the ground started shaking beneath their feet. They again looked up into the sky and again they saw not one, but *two* suns blazing in the sky. Then came the thunderous boom that rocked the entire Middle East; beyond Jordan and beyond Syria, over the nation of Israel, the neighbor to Palestine.

The Palestinian was the first to fall to his knees. "No...no...Nooo!" he cried. "*ASTAGFU-RALLAH! AZZA WA JAL! INNA LILLAHI WA INNA ILAYHI RAJIUN!*"

The American stood dazedly, "Oh my God," he said, "Oh my God…"

The blooming cloud from the explosion expanded upward into the sky, and emerging out from the smoke beneath the cloud, both men saw a brightly-lit winged orb that accelerated into the sky, toward one of the suns, faster than anything he had ever seen.

The final journal entry was written by the Palestinian:

> *I hear music in my mind. Old songs. Ancient hymns. I now recognize them as the songs of my soul. Desert songs…for only being out here have I come to listen to them, to listen to the restless peace in me, begging to be heard, but yearning to know what will become of it.*

> *I know this cannot be a day when I shall be judged harshly, because I can still hear this music; I can still hear the peace in its melody, carrying me off to distant memories and lands I've not yet been in this body, but have often visited in my dreams. A vision of my brother*

flashed before me. Then of my sister, Sanaa... she was looking past me...as though looking for my American friend behind me.

It will not be long now, when we both take our last gasp. I am glad to be with a man whom I once called my enemy, who is now my friend...my brother. We now know why we survived, and we leave you with these words to find and discover. We have witnessed what we were supposed to witness, the cosmic event and the great cloud and tremor; the sackcloth of the living, set off, as these experiences have taught me, in ignorance and foolery. However, a flower somewhere will still open; a baby will still cry, and smiles will still be born from love. And peace, I am now confident, will one day thrive. Yes, peace is coming...it is near, on the great, majestic horizon.

I again think of my brother. We shall be re-united soon. I think of my father. I hope he has forgiven me. But it is in deep, pure love I know, when all is forgiven – that love we feel upon death; upon Heaven…we take it with us.

The American's breathing is slow and weak now, like my own. With little strength he has left, I heard him utter to his parents – sending his words to the sky and to me, so I may set them down here: "I love you, Mom. I love you, Dad. Thank you for my life. I got my glory, Dad…I found my glory. I am at peace. I have learned so much these last few days…so much. Peace is possible. Lose your perceptions and start over. We know nothing. Stop listening to everyone else. Listen to yourselves. Find your own truth, and come together. Don't let governments and secret groups divide you. Love you all…" May his loved ones and the world feel his heart in every word.

I must go now. Allah and God…the supreme being of all humanity, wished us to tell you our story, and now we have. The question now becomes…what will you do with it? How will you use it? Or will you at all? Do not weep, but rejoice, for in these last days we have lived and experienced and felt the magic that not ten lives do see. From both of us: Ma Salama! God Bless! Farewell…we are now one. Our energy is in the air that you breathe.

During the days of these two men, the notion of war, at the onset, always seemed to possess some unseen valiance, however the actuality and reality of it, despite the apparent heroics, was one of the saddest and most tragic episodes in the human concourse. As we have come to know, it is a lesson of how *not* to exist.

War used to be a commentary on the state of a nation; how unified it was, the measure of its spirit and strength, and where it stood in the hearts of the world's people. However, this commentary rarely dictated the livelihood of war, nor did it justify its immeasurable pains; it did not diminish war's savagery, nor increase its righteousness.

Theirs was an age when, in positions of power, there were more mice than men.

I have tried to give you the best account I could of these two men's journey and amazing end. There was more in each of them than anything that could ever be in the desert – that *was* in the desert. I hope I have succeeded and served you well.

May the story of these men inspire millions toward peace and love. May their story inspire you, for *anything* is possible. Believe…and you shall receive. And to my dear brother: I Love you. Thank you for *you*. May you hold the hands of our Mother and Father in Heaven, until that hour comes when I can join you, and we shall all unite again.

And the Lord said unto Moses, How long will this people provoke me? And how long will it be ere they believe me, for all the signs which I have shewed among them? I will smite them with pestilence, and disinherit them, and will make of thee a greater nation and mightier than they...as for you, your carcasses, they shall fall in this wilderness. And your children shall wander in the wilderness forty years, and bear your whoredoms, until your carcasses be wasted in the wilderness... I the Lord have said, I will surely do it unto all this evil congregation, that are gathered together against me: in this wilderness they shall be consumed, and there they shall die.

-- The Old Testament
Numbers 14; 11,12,32,33,35

In the name of Allah, Most Gracious, Most Merciful. By the steeds that run, with panting breath, And strike sparks of fire, And push home the charge in the morning, And raise the dust in clouds the while, And penetrate forthwith into the midst of the foe en masse; Truly Man is to his Lord ungrateful; And to that fact He bears witness by his deeds; And he is violent in his love of wealth. Does he not know, when that which is in the graves is scattered abroad And that which is locked up in human breasts is made manifest That their Lord had been well-acquainted with them even to that day?

-- The Koran, Surah 100
Al 'Adiyat, or Those that run

About the Author

NEAL BOGOSIAN is the author of *The Age of Healing: Profiles from an Energy Healer*, and the young adult baseball novel, *The Adventures of Chip Doolin*. He is a former Special Education teacher, and holds a double Master's Degree in Education. He lives in Rhode Island, where he has maintained a holistic healing practice since 2010.

Made in United States
North Haven, CT
27 August 2022

23362283R00136